The Vagueness of the Tropics

and Other Stories

Miguel Antonio Ortiz

Irene Weinberger Books
an imprint of Hamilton Stone Editions
Maplewood, New Jersey

Graphics by Miguel Antonio Ortiz

Library of Congress Cataloging-in-Publication Data

Names: Ortiz, Miguel Antonio, author.
Title: The vagueness of the tropics and other stories / Miguel Antonio Ortiz.
Description: Maplewood, New Jersey : Irene Weinberger Books, [2021] |
Summary: "The Vagueness of the Tropics and other stories is a collection of literary short stories by Miguel Antonio Ortiz, the author of several other novels and collections as well as books for children"-- Provided by publisher.
Identifiers: LCCN 2021008064 | ISBN 9780979598685 (trade paperback)
Subjects: LCGFT: Short stories.
Classification: LCC PS3615.R825 V34 2021 | DDC 813/.6--dc23
LC record available at https://lccn.loc.gov/2021008064

Contents

The Vagueness of the Tropics

MARIE AND HARRY had arranged to meet in the sculpture garden at the Museum of Modern Art, and sitting in the courtyard, they observed a photographer and a model using the stone artwork as background for a series of photos. Walking briskly, the model approached three slabs of polished stone that protruded diagonally from the terrace floor. She then turned her head abruptly as if suddenly arrested by the glistening black surfaces of the three symmetrical shapes. The procedure was repeated several times while the photographer, with a flick of his finger, fixed the passing image into permanent pixels.

"What have you been up to?" Marie asked.

"I've been loafing," Harry answered, his face beaming, as if, under the circumstances, that was a witty response. He was reluctant to give an account of his futile attempts to render time unimportant.

A soft blue sky jutted out from behind the tall buildings that surrounded the garden. Looking up they both observed the contrast of styles that hemmed them in. The glass facades reflected multiple shades of subtle hues, while brick and masonry, casting hard shadows, formed intricate geometrical patterns.

"For the first time I'm completely free," he said.

"Are you?" she skeptically questioned.

"Yes, I don't owe anybody anything." He paused, and then added, "Well, almost, I work for my father, if one can call that work."

"What else can you call it?"

"I haven't decided. I'm not quite sure what he expects. Ivan Cosme and Son, Civil Engineers, he gets a kick out of that."

"I have no certainties either. That's being too free."

It would have been useless, he assumed, to suggest ways for her to acquire responsibilities, except that of rescuing him from his predicament. But that was out of the question, something that would both shock her and put him in the ungraceful position of a suppliant. Besides, if she were seeking his help, as he suspected, it would be a betrayal to dwell on his own quandary. Betrayal of whom or what—he was uncertain. There was an imprecise connection between his interests and hers. Above all, he did not wish anything awkward to occur. He prized style, the art of seeming naturalness, and he preferred to wait for the appropriate moment, the mark of what he considered good taste. That approach, he was convinced, provided better results.

It had been so when they first met in college. He recalled waiting for something to happen, waiting for her to become real. He had memories of her gracefulness, of whispers, of grey tones accentuated here and there by the dark woodwork of the student lounge where the moment had occurred. Everything was vague except the impression that something special had happened, something that made them less than strangers, though it was long after they had first met. He did not remember what they had been talking about, but he had the distinct impression that something had taken place.

A mist enveloped everything that preceded that moment, and disconnected scenes were the most he discerned of previous years. He recalled the plump girl, in the blue serape

and fishnet stockings, who had introduced them. In the morning sunlight, the three of them stood by a window in the hallway of the student center. Marie's wide forehead and soft brown eyes riveted him. The plump girl in the serape chatted about the psychology of rats. Marie turned her head to gaze at the trees in the courtyard, the branches covered with tender shoots that would soon burst into full bloom; on the ground, those that had been blown down by the wind formed a sparse green carpet. "Yes, but what of…" he was saying to the girl in blue, while he listened to laughing voices receding down the hallway. His eyes followed the contour of Marie's profile. Then he too gazed at the trees in the courtyard.

The summer after graduation she left for Europe and did not return in the Fall. Eventually self-doubt tinted his memory. He wondered whether he had merely observed a mask of youth. Still, everything need not have been lost. One morning, at sunrise, in a motel at Old Orchard Beach in Maine, he left his traveling companion in bed and took a walk along the water. The sight of tumultuous clouds hanging over a horizon of limitless ocean awoke in him a feeling of astonishment, as if that vast panorama existed within him, and he was for the first time gazing upon himself. He wanted her there then. He listened to the shrieks of the sea gulls and the hoarse murmuring of the surf and wished that he might decipher their message. Three years later, running into her in the street, he was immediately taken by the change. He saw right away that she too was aware of it.

Now, in sculpture the garden, she had an enigmatic smile, as if she were amused by a subtle pain. "Why did you not follow me to Europe?" she asked.

The question seemed a displaced concept, a stranger in his universe. "Why didn't I follow you?" he repeated astounded.

"I never quite understood your reason for opting out."

He saw a glimmer of her former self. She was perfectly serious, but he felt like the object of a practical joke. He did not recall having been presented with the option, and he had failed to provide it on his own.

"You might have returned at the end of the summer. I might have come back with you," she said.

The orderly layout of the garden began to oppress him. The rectilinear motif was too controlled, the gurgling in the rectangular fountain too gentle, and the trees and shrubs too flimsy. The regulated effect was at odds with the tumult within him. The thundering of imagined surf drowned the rustling of the leaves. The spinning in his head rendered insignificant the swaying of the sculpture that towered over them.

"You might have helped me," she continued.

"I would have only stood in your way," he said without believing his own words.

"I did the same over there as I was doing here. I couldn't extricate myself."

Unprepared to see tears streak down her cheeks, he merely observed in silence.

"I was sliding from one day to the next without purpose. I thought a change of scene would help, would make me different."

He sensed a door opening for him—a chance to make amends. But he merely asked. "What now?"

"I'm going to Costa Rica. There…"

"Why would Costa Rica succeed where Europe failed?"

"It's different down there. There I may encounter the primitive."

"For that there are better places ..."

"Costa Rica appeals to me."

A host of platitudes came to mind, but he dismissed them. He felt an inner disturbance, as if she had casually thrown a pebble into a still pool where the unwelcomed ripples would soon subside.

"Come with me," she added.

"To Costa Rica?"

"Yes, to Costa Rica, with me."

Salvation beckoned him, but he felt caught in a dream where his feet moved without propelling him. He wanted to lunge forward, to accept, but instead he asked, "When are you leaving?"

"Next week."

"I don't know," he said.

"You can think it over."

"I may not be able to settle my affairs in so short a time."

"You can meet me there later."

"I'll think about it."

He had obligations. He had a career that had not really been his choice, but what would he get for abandoning it?

"Think it over," she repeated.

"I will," he vaguely rejoined as he imagined her disappearing into the vagueness of the tropics.

City Snips

THE CITY HAS a distinct character, and each neighborhood has its own flavor. My wife and I, Brooklynites, often see movies at the Brooklyn Academy Cinema. On a Saturday afternoon, waiting for show time, she decided to make a pit stop. I stayed in my seat and overheard a conversation between a man and a woman sitting behind me. The man was to marry soon, and they were discussing the approaching event.

"It's interesting," the woman said, "how you knew right off that she was the one. I too immediately sensed that she was the one for you."

"She and I see eye-to-eye on so many things. Sometimes we don't even have to talk to know what the other is thinking."

"Have you decided where you're going to live?"

"We haven't seriously discussed it," he said. "I assume that at first we'll live in my apartment, though we'll move to the suburbs eventually. I don't want to raise children in the city." After a pause, he followed with, "She wants to keep a kosher home, and I said to her, 'Then, I won't be able to make my paella.'"

"Ah, and you make such good paella," said his companion.

"But we worked out a solution," he said. "I can still make paella, but we'll eat it on paper plates."

"Oh, is that allowed?"

"Sure," said the man. "My mother kept a kosher home, and when we ordered pizza or Chinese food, we ate on paper plates."

At that point, my Jewish wife returned and began to talk to me. Her voice drowned out the conversation behind us.

Clearly, overhearing conversations of city people makes a rather interesting pastime. At The Strand I was looking through the books on the bargain book table when two women approached in search of a particular title.

As they perused the display, the first woman said in a thick Russian accent, “The book was here the other day. I know you’ll like it.” Soon enough she spied what she was searching for. “Here it is,” she exclaimed, reaching for *Like Water for Chocolate*. “It’s like a Mexican soap opera,” she gleefully explained, as she handed the book to her companion.

Her friend perused the book, and then passed it back. “No,” she said in her heavy accent, “I think it would bore me.”

A look of disappointment invaded the first woman’s face and, silently, she put the book down.

The Strand provides a very particular atmosphere and is a cultural niche. Likewise 47th Street between Fifth and Sixth Avenues, the jewelry district as some call it, has a flavor of its own. I went there one day looking to buy a silver chain for my wife. I had bought her one the year before, but she had recently lost it. The loss upset her. I figured replacing the chain would make a good Christmas present, a nice chain at a reasonable price. I intended to go back to the place where I had bought the original one, but I couldn’t exactly remember which vendor had sold it to me. I recalled that it was at the back of one of the large exchanges on the south side of the street, a very brightly lit booth with a great deal of glass, and a column going right through the counter. I figured if I went into the larger places I was bound to find it.

The first three places I went into had no booths that resembled the one I was looking for. I spotted a booth with a black man behind the counter, an unusual sight in the jewelry district, where most vendors are white and Jewish. I asked him about silver chains, and he directed me to the next booth. The woman there smiled.

"I'm looking for a silver chain about thirty inches long," I said.

"For a man or woman?"

"For my wife."

The saleswoman brought out several chains. I examined them, trying to compare each to my memory of the lost one. The ones I picked up all seemed to weigh less than the one I remembered. "Do you have any that are heavier?" I asked.

She brought out a heavier one, but it wasn't as nice as the ones already on display. "The thinner ones are nicer for a lady," she said.

"How much is this one?" I asked choosing the one I thought was most like the lost one.

The saleswoman measured the chain and weighed it. "Forty-five dollars," she said.

That was twenty dollars more than I had paid for the original. I pretended to consider it, then asked for her card and left. Out on the street I walked to the next building. It was a smaller exchange. I walked straight to the back, and lo and behold, there it was, the very booth I had been looking for. I went straight to the spot where I had stood the first time. The proprietor was talking to another man, but this time there was a young woman there also, and she immediately came over to help me. She had a distinct non-European look, but I couldn't determine any particular racial or national origin.

"I'm interested in a thirty inch silver chain," I said.

She brought out a greater variety of chains than I had been shown at the other place, including one exactly like the one for which I had been quoted a price. There was a more elaborate chain, which I also liked, but I thought my wife might think it too ornate. She had said she wanted a simple chain. I asked the price of the one that looked the same as the one I had seen at the other place. The young woman weighed the chain and said, "Twenty-four dollars."

"I'll take it," I said. I gave her a twenty-dollar bill and a five. She obtained change from the proprietor, and she handed me the dollar.

"Would you like a box?"

"Yes, please," I said.

She put the chain in a little box and the box into a bag, and handed it to me.

"Have a very good day," she said.

"Thank you, you have a good day also," I said.

I was having a very good day. On my way back to the office, I tried to figure out why the first woman had tried to overcharge me. Did I look like a sucker? Had I behaved in a way that said, "Please fleece me"? I think the key was having asked for a heavier chain. At that point she must have figured that I wanted to spend more, and that if she tried to sell me a chain for only twenty-four dollars, I would think it was not substantial enough and would not buy it. She gambled that I did not know the price of silver, but luckily that was my second time buying a silver chain.

I was reminded of the time I had bought my wife a gold chain also, on 47th Street. At the counter, the saleswoman showed me a very unusual gold chain. "Made in Italy," she said, "all our jewelry comes from Italy."

I was delighted that the gold chain was only three hundred and fifty dollars. While the salesperson was wrapping it up another woman, who was visibly older, spoke to her in a language I did not understand, not Italian. The conversation was obviously about the transaction. The older woman became upset. I deduced from the tone of her voice that the price was in dispute. The younger woman had sold it for too little. Not that they were taking a loss, but that the older more experienced woman had judged, correctly, that I would have paid more for the chain, but it was too late then. Luck had been with me that day also.

The subway too offers distinct possibilities. Yesterday I encountered a young woman whom I usually see at the Vanderbilt Y when I go there at lunchtime to exercise. I had seen her once walking along Prospect Park South, so the next time I saw her at the Y, I spoke to her. She's very pretty, but very young and not yet very comfortable with herself. She lacks the poise that comes with self-confidence, but she's trying hard to acquire it. She works for Harper & Row in the children's books division.

She got on the train at Fourth Avenue, though she had told me, when I had first met her, that she lives in Windsor

Terrace. Maybe she moved. I looked up from my book and there she was standing in front of me. We both smiled at the same time. She sat next to me, though there were plenty of other seats available that morning. I took that as a friendly sign. At the Y we had not spoken since that first time several months before, so I was sure that she had no interest in further acquaintance. She was holding a book, and I asked her what she was reading. She showed me the cover, very bright and illustrated in a cartoon style. It cried out literature for young people. It was by a woman author unknown to me.

"I haven't read anything by her," I said.

"And why not? She's a terrific writer."

"I'll make a note of that," I said.

"There's a lot of talk about books in this story. It makes me very happy," she said. "What are you reading?"

I showed her the spine of the book I was holding, *Barchester Towers*. "Old stuff," I said.

She agreed.

We both went back to our books, but it took me a while to refocus on what I was reading. I had to read the same page three times before I was able to continue.

Empty Cup

"YOU KNOW," **Bella** said, "it's not a step to be taken lightly. Nowadays people think it's such an easy thing to get a divorce that getting married in haste doesn't matter. It's done or undone so easily, but it shouldn't be like that."

"It's a crying shame," Maryellen agreed as she limped across the kitchen carrying the tray of silver she meant to polish that day. She wore a loose-fitting cotton dress. Her white hair came down just above her shoulders. Her face was relatively smooth for someone her age. Her blue eyes were clear and devoid of mystery. As if she had had an uneventful life, nothing of momentous consequence showed on her face. "Young people don't understand," Maryellen said. "It's nothing to them."

"If one could only pass one's experience on to one's children," Bella lamented.

"That would be a feat," Maryellen said. "That would be better than leaving them money. But you can't mix experience in with their food, and whatever you say goes in one ear and out the other. That's the truth. It's the same as when we were young. We didn't listen to our parents either, did we? We knew everything back then. It took us a while to find out how much we didn't know. It would have gone so much easier if we had listened."

"Maybe for some," Bella said skeptically, "but that wasn't the case with me." She sipped her coffee while silently debating whether she wanted to have this conversation with Maryellen, who was, after all, merely her employee. She had learned as a child that the workers did not eat at the same table as their employers, else what was the sense of having them. Bella believed that she had outgrown that. Why should she spend her time polishing the silver, when she could pay someone else to do it? It was simply that and nothing else, she told herself, not about feeling superior because she could pay, as had been the implication from her elders. There was no sense either, she thought, in going to the other extreme—of not having any help at all because it was not right to have other people pick up after one. That was a point of view, absurd as it sounded, of some people nowadays. There was still the question of keeping one's distance. But that was altogether a different matter. That had only to do with making life easier, not just for herself but for Maryellen also, or for anybody in a similar situation.

"I was married to Henry for thirty-five years," she said deciding against caution. What could she reveal to Maryellen that she had not already surmised? Pretense was all that might be lost, and at this stage, that was expendable.

Maryellen continued to polish the silver without giving any indication of whether she was aware of the crossing of any Rubicon on Bella's part. Bella was grateful for that nicety whether it was intentional or not.

"Thirty-five years is a good chunk of time," Maryellen said in a matter-of-fact voice.

"What could I have done differently?" Bella asked as if the facts formulated in that way were an indictment of her life.

Maryellen looked up from her task, startled for a moment. She searched Bella's face for some indication that the question was rhetorical, but finding none, she chose to ignore it. It was the best she could do in good conscience, since she had no way of arriving at a rational answer.

Indeed, there was nothing that Bella could have done differently then, or so it seemed to her now. She would have had to have been a different person than she was then. She would have had to have been at the very least the person whom she now was, or very nearly so in spirit. This was an essential problem of hindsight, a pitfall: the belief that looking back one saw oneself, when in fact what one saw was a distant predecessor of the self one had become.

So now Bella looked back to a time when she had been but a girl under the influence a smothering family. The person she had been then was but the seed, the potentiality, of the person she was now. She recalled one spring evening walking hand in hand with a boy down the park path through the blossoming cherry trees. She remembered the boy with curly black hair and intense eyes who begged her to consider his affection.

"I doubted myself," Bella said, "and the result was thirty-five years of a miserable marriage."

"Was it bad at the beginning?" Maryellen asked.

"It was bad from day one. It was bad even from before that."

"There was no love, then?" Maryellen asked.

It was not an easy question for Bella to answer, though the answer was apparent. It was difficult to accept the facts as she perceived them—to own up to them so unequivocally.

The questions, like a spotlight aimed at a dark corner full of forms vague enough to allow for interpretation, suddenly revealed objects in full detail. Memory is replete with such nooks that allow selective illumination to mitigate the discomfort of unpleasant recollections.

"I was in love once," she said, "but not with Henry."

She remembered the boy with intense eyes and curly black hair under the cherry blossoms in the park. She remembered his face close to hers, and how she closed her eyes when their lips met. She did not now remember the smell of him, after so many years, but she remembered remembering that it had had an extraordinary effect on her, and for a long time after, the remembrance of the texture of his lips and the smell of him so intoxicated her that she was afraid that she would unintentionally betray herself. She was never again able to achieve that feeling, with Henry or with anybody else. She could not even remember the feeling now, but only that she had cherished it. It was but a memory of a memory, the shadow of a shadow.

"It might have been different had I married him," she said. Indeed it might have been different, it would have been different, but what the difference would have been was too great to comprehend. There was the pain, of course, to use as a reference. She had lived with it for so long not knowing what it was, not knowing even that it existed. It had revealed itself to her by its effects. She had discovered it like an astronomer might discover an unseen astral phenomenon, some black hole that defies detection by light oriented instruments, or a planet always presenting its dark side, but nevertheless bending objects to it gravitational force. So now she tried to imagine what life would have been without it, without the burden, the effects of so massive an object in the universe of emotions. Imagination failed her. Though she was now in some sense free of the oppressive body, it had for so long dominated every aspect of her life that she could not reconstruct what the past might have been but in the most general terms.

"Why didn't you?" Maryellen asked in absentminded relentlessness.

Bella drew a deep breath, as if the answer to that question laid at the bottom of a deep lagoon into which she was prepared to dive to retrieve it. "To put it simply," she said, "he was my cousin." She was up too soon to have plumbed the depth of the matter.

"I see," Maryellen said almost carelessly. "One doesn't want those kinds of problems."

"No, one doesn't," Bella agreed, "but I didn't care, you see. It wasn't a concern to me."

"You didn't plan to have children?"

"I didn't plan anything," she said, "One doesn't plan at times like those."

"I suppose not," Maryellen conceded. She was for the moment left dangling, but she was now aware that Bella was out to make a point, that she would do it whether prodded or not, and in all probability better if she were left to her own cadence.

"It was my mother," Bella said, "who opposed it most vehemently." She paused for a moment, then added, "I have always thought she meant well."

The "always" struck Maryellen as excessive, but it was not her place to contradict. It was not, after all, refinement of her style that Bella was looking for, if she was looking for anything at all. Where Bella was going had become a question for Maryellen, and she took it on as a responsibility to assist Bella in finding her way there. That would have presupposed that Maryellen knew where "there" was, but that was not the case. What she knew was that Bella was bent on going, rather on getting there, for she had already gone, that is, had started out for some destination without having, Maryellen suspected, any clear idea of how to get there.

"It was a concern to your parents," Maryellen said.

"And to his," Bella added with some emphasis. "They were all arrayed against us." It had been overwhelming the "all"—a solid marshalling of family against the two youths. She recalled the despair of having no one in authority to turn to, no one to take their side, to render aid or comfort—like facing a precipice with foothold difficult to find. The task was daunting.

"And so you married Mr. Thompson instead."

"That's the long and short of it," she said. "He was the darling of everyone. How could I resist?"

"Your life would have been different with your cousin," Maryellen said, "but not necessarily better."

"I'll never know, will I?"

"No, you'll never know."

"The problem is," Bella explained. "I can't imagine a different bad life, only the opposite of what I had."

"Well, what became of your cousin? Did he marry?"

"Yes, he married eventually I heard. He's a veterinarian in Montana, or he was. Perhaps he's retired by now."

"Is that a life you would have wanted?"

"He loved horses."

"What about you?"

"I loved him," she said simply as if that encompassed all possibilities.

"I was married too," Maryellen said.

"Were you?"

"Long ago, almost too long to remember," Maryellen said. "But my case was quite different from yours, not in outcome, in its beginning. I married whom I wanted, and he turned out to be a bum. I got rid of him quick enough, and it cured me of ever wanting to be married again."

"It was fortunate, then, that you came to your senses when you were still young. You didn't have any children, did you?"

"That's my one regret."

"Don't regret. You escaped a lot of heartache."

"I had heartaches aplenty, just not about children."

"Nothing compares to your own children for giving you heartaches," Bella said, at last approaching the destination for which she had set out. The tension drained from her face as if the words relieved her of a burden, but the change was only momentary. The hard lines soon began to reappear as she contemplated the conundrum created by her own daughter's desire to marry. She cut herself short, knowing that the marrying was not the problem, but rather marrying the wrong person. Still, that was not it. She was moving in concentric circles to the heart of the matter. "How does one know what right is?" she asked out loud, not really addressing the question to her companion.

Maryellen nevertheless picked up. "Oh, I knew what wrong was after six months. Rather that's when I decided there was no hope. I can see him now sneaking into the bedroom at two o'clock in the morning. He had his cap in his hand, and he tiptoed in looking towards the bed where he hoped I was fast asleep. I can still see the cherubic face with the thin moustache over his lip, thinking he could put one over on me. 'A night out with the boys,' he said. I could smell the perfume all over him."

"Yes, but you didn't know it before that. How could one know before hand?"

"My mother, bless her soul, she knew. She warned me, but I didn't listen."

"But what if she'd been wrong?"

"That's always the question, 'what if?'"

"My mother was wrong," Bella said, "and I ended up with Henry."

"That was long ago," Maryellen said.

"Yes, and now there's Frannie. What do I do about Frannie?"

What to do about Frannie was always the question that hung over Bella, the overwhelming role that descended on her after the birth of her daughter. It had been a blessed event indeed, letting her slip out of the growingly odious role of wife into the more acceptable one of mother. Acceptable of course did not mean comfortable, for it was something she had, like all mothers, to constantly reinvent. Every step of the child's development presented a new set of problems and questions that forced a reassessment of the old and ever present puzzle. It was not comfortable for Bella to be constantly wrestling with the question of what to do, in a sense, how to be a parent—having over and over to learn the role anew. It did however allow her, if not to escape completely, to keep at a greater distance whatever was left of her matrimonial feelings.

It was inevitable that she would want to look back at her own upbringing for clues that would, like a mariner's chart, warn her of the approaching depths and shallows, the changing tides, the treacherous currents and possible sheltering headlands and harbors in this journey where her duty was to deliver her cargo safely to the shores of adulthood. The looking back also had been, and still was, a problem for Bella, being well aware of the failures of her own mother's efforts. She was now confronted with the next stretch of the journey, perhaps the most treacherous, in that she had to relinquish control, which to that point she had theoretically held. It was at this point that her parents had failed; or at least, where the failure had been most blatant. That they had not let her choose, she could never forget, which in this case amounted to never forgive. Bella was fixed on that incident as the one that doomed her, but that was only the culmination of a long series of actions that rendered her incapable of choosing a path other than the one prescribed by authority.

The fear that she might do to Frannie what was done to her was a thought that clouded Bella's life. Consciously or not, she had raised Frannie to be her own person, and Frannie would do what she would do, as Bella well knew, regardless of what anyone else advised.

"I certainly see your problem," Maryellen said.

"Do you really?" Bella perked up, an expression of anticipation suddenly breaking out over her face. The "seeing" of a problem was, after all, the beginning of arriving at a solution, and the fact that Maryellen could see, admitted that she saw, was a sign that the matter was not hopeless.

"Well," Maryellen continued, "must you do anything?"

"I can let her do whatever she wants, which is what I always do. But then what becomes of my obligation as a mother?"

"What indeed?"

"I know she's making a mistake."

"Do you?"

"I can feel it in my bones."

"It's her mistake to make."

"Yes, but it's my duty to warn her."

"That shouldn't be too difficult."

"On the contrary. It's the most difficult thing to do, just because it does seem so simple. She will ignore the simple. She will have anticipated it and already discarded it. The trick is to warn her in a way she is not expecting. It has to be creative and subtle. Oh, how I hate that word, 'creative.' It's not simple at all."

"It certainly isn't," Maryellen said. She put down the utensil she had just finished polishing and picked up another.

Bella waited for Maryellen to continue. Now that they had established that something different was in order, Bella hoped that her employee would come up with a useful suggestion. It was only a hope, but as the seconds progressed, it very dangerously approached expectation. It was perhaps a sign of desperation that the lady was casting about in areas of the stream she would have normally considered unpromising, as if the sun being low in the sky, the angler having to face the necessity of soon calling it day, and not yet having anything to show for the long hours of casting into the still and shaded pools near the shore, was now moving out to where the water ran faster in the desperate hope that perversity in this case would pay off as the exception that proves the rule.

Maryellen, however, was silent, and Bella was left to wonder what had caused her to draw back when moments before she had seemed on the brink of providing so much of the longed for aid. "I have no idea, you know, where to go from here," Bella said, words that were as much of a direct appeal as she could muster. The fact that she would venture even that was a surprise to Maryellen, on whom the significance of the plea was not lost, although she did not immediately make any visible acknowledgement of it.

"The idea, you know," Maryellen said finally, "is not for you to go anywhere, but to let her come to you."

"Yes, but how on earth is one to manage that?"

"That's just it," Maryellen said, "you don't manage. The whole matter will manage itself. All you have to do is wait."

"I suppose I have no choice," Bella said.

"Of course you do," Maryellen replied. "The whole point is that you do choose. You choose to wait. If you don't choose it, then you're not waiting."

"What them am I doing?" Bella asked.

"I don't know, but not waiting. At least not the kind of waiting that's required. You must wait with a purpose."

Bella took that in, but tried as she would to process what Maryellen was trying to convey, she could not. Like making gelatin in a refrigerator that was not cold enough, the liquid would not congeal. "I don't know, Maryellen," Bella said, "I don't see it the way you do."

"It takes some getting used to," Maryellen said. "Maybe you need to sleep on it."

"Maybe I do," Bella said, "Maybe I do."

Looking down into her cup of coffee, she saw that it was empty.

On Monday

THE FIRST TIME, Enrique wasn't sure of what he saw. They were quite a distance away, and he relied mainly on their outline and on what he thought was their distinctive gait. They were gone by the time he reached a spot close enough to make a definite identification.

He couldn't call it a betrayal, because no one had given him a pledge, and neither had he made one. He tried to be rational. After all, Bryan did not know how he felt about Anna. In front of his friends, he always had treated her with the utmost casualness.

He had assumed, however, she was aware of all the nuances of the situation. Yet that too was unfair, since he had not offered her anything. He had only given her the space she required, but he had done that not just for her benefit but for his also. He had been well aware of what he was doing, and he had assumed that she too was aware, but now, that belief became questionable. If she knew what she meant to him, she would not be so insensitive as to pick up with his close friend.

"Jesus Christ, look at you," his cousin, Joanna, said, "You're falling apart."

"I'm alright," he said.

"No, you're not," she said. "You have to do something."

"There's nothing I can do."

"You have to tell Bryan what the situation is."

"I can't do that," he said. "It wouldn't be fair."

"What the hell does that mean?"

"It would create a dilemma for him."

"So what?"

"It wouldn't be right."

"Why not?"

"It just wouldn't."

"He'd put you on the spot?"

"He wouldn't. He wouldn't have too."

"So you have to play by his rules? This is some kind of a macho thing isn't it?"

"I don't know what that means."

"You have to tell Anna then."

"I can't."

"Why not?"

"She's entitled to what she wants."

"What about you? What are you entitled to?"

Without an answer to that question, he stared at her blankly.

"And anyway how do you know what she wants, if you don't give her an option? Maybe this isn't about what she wants; this is about what you want. You have to talk to her. Then she can decide."

"You don't understand," he said.

"I understand that you're stuck on some weird set of rules that don't make any sense," she said.

He could not find the words to express the dilemma that confronted both Anna and him—each trying to make an escape that might be hindered by the other. Only someone in a similar situation would understand. Anna would know immediately what he was feeling, just as he knew her predicament and her fear. He was trying to get to the other side of a river, while swimming against the current. It wasn't the fault of the river. The current bore him no malice. It was flowing down to the sea just like every river current does. If his destination was upstream, it was nobody's fault. It was just the way things were. By a quirk of fate, he had arrived at the river downstream from his goal.

"I'm afraid," he said, "that if I hook up with Anna I will be doing what I'm expected to do. I will be flowing with the current, and I'll end up where I don't want to be."

"You want to be with her, don't you?"

"Yes, with her, but there's more to her than her person. I'm sure that she feels the same way about me. It would be too easy for each of us to conform to the expectations of our families if we are together. My mother and hers would become friends and team up against us."

"Your mother is a saint, and she wouldn't do anything against you."

"She is, but saints have their own agendas. My mother wants only good for me, but her vision of what's good is limited by her own experience. I will never be able to explain to her what I'm doing, and where I want to go."

"You're selling her short."

"Maybe I am, but can I afford to take a chance?"

"If this struggle of yours is so difficult don't you think you could use an ally, someone who understands it as well as you do? Anna is the ideal person. She would be a help rather than a hindrance. Since you're both in the same predicament, she would work with you on the problem."

He had already considered that possibility. He wished

that it were only so—that he could wallow in the comfort of having her. She understood his dreams and fears—the fears that came to him just before sleep every night. In childhood, he had been able to ward them off with prayers. They were different fears now, no less terrifying, but he no longer had the talisman of prayer. The fear was an overwhelming loneliness, dark, pervasive, impervious to reality. The fear took no notice of the many people he consorted with all day long. It didn't care about his cafeteria friends, nor about his family. They don't exist, the fear told him. They don't exist in your soul.

Enrique looked for his soul and he could not find it. How could that be? Wasn't it like his shadow—something that could not be misplaced? He desperately needed help in finding it. The image of Anna insinuated itself into his dreams as he retreated into sleep. *The jingle of his spurs rang loudly as he walked towards the cabin at the bottom of the hill. Wisps of smoke drifted skyward from the tubular chimney with a conical top. Someone was surely in there, and the sound of the spurs was sure to warn them of the approaching figure dressed all in black with silver trimming—the gun slung low on his right side, his arm relaxed, his fingers limber and ready to spring into action. The noise of the spurs did not alarm him. He wanted his enemies to hear him approach. The sound of his footsteps would instill fear in their hearts. Fear was his ally. The Kid paused before the grey weather beaten door. He could turn around and walk away and spare himself the trouble of killing his enemies, but it would only be a postponement. Sooner or later he would have to face them. There was no way to avoid the inevitable. The enmity between the Kid and his opponents could not be ignored. They were relentless and implacable. Best to walk in right away and get it over with. The Kid felt only a slight quickening of his heart as he swung the door open with the tip of his boot. There was no flash of gunfire—only the darkness of the inner cabin as his eyes adjusted to the absence of sunlight.*

"You have come at last," a voice addressed him from a corner of the dark room. The Kid was surprised by its sweetness. He turned, all the time ready to draw his six-shooter, but there was no need. It was only Anna.

He remembered his dream with longing, and he said to Joanna, "You're right. I must tell her."

But his resolve failed him. A week later nothing had changed. Everything was proceeding according to the usual script. Bryan had invited Anna for the weekend to his parents' house in the country.

"So did you tell her?" Joanna asked.

"I didn't have the nerve," he said.

"You don't know what it's like," he said to Joanna. "I wait every day by Finnley Hall hoping to run into her between classes. I pretend to be just hanging out or just sitting around trying to do my homework on the steps. All that happens is that I look at the text and remember nothing. From a long way off I recognize her. I know her posture and her gait, so I know it's her, long before I see her face. Every day I intend to confront her, but every day I keep my nose in the book as she passes by. If I raise my eyes to meet hers, she waves to me, but I do nothing. On Thursday it was raining. The dampness threatened to seep through my jacket even after I retreated to the library portico. She scurried by under a dark umbrella, but I didn't follow her as I had intended. There was no huddling under the umbrella in tearful revelations, no damp embrace that would make the coldness of the rain irrelevant. It's no use."

"Yes, you're hopeless. What stopped you? What have you got to lose?"

"I have her to lose," he said.

His own words startled him, because she was not his to lose, or so it seemed at the moment. He was compelled look more closely, but what he saw was not altogether clear. He had a claim of some kind, but he could not define it in absolute terms. It was something he felt, but that was not enough. He had too long been immersed in an objectivist world, so that he had almost lost touch with another and just as useful way perceiving. It was a dangerous way that required more skill and more discipline to employ successfully. It was necessary and not to be replaced by the common.

"You have to protect her from your predatory friend," Joanna said.

"Is that all? It has to be more than that."

"Yes, so go with it," she admonished

"I never felt the need to protect anybody else from him."

"Precisely, so now is your chance to make amends."

"But isn't it up to the buyer to beware? If women don't see beyond his superficial charm, it's because they don't want to. What they get is exactly what he offers, charm and a good time. Ultimately that's not enough, but it's a lesson to be learned just as much as the causes of the Civil War or the conditions leading to Reformation. It's not for me to teach the lesson—not even to Anna. If I try, I don't think she will listen? I hoped that she was different, and maybe she is. She may have a reason of her own to ignore a warning. It might be that she knows exactly what she is getting into—that she has prepared the lesson for herself, and it is something other than what I imagined."

"Well, it's up to you, and if you want let him go unchallenged, there's nothing more I can say."

That conclusion was no comfort to him. He slept badly that Friday night. Getting through Saturday and Sunday would be the hardest part. He would be all right on Monday, he told himself.

Birds of One Kind or Another

AFTER LUNCH, WE were still sitting at El Gallito, when a young man walked directly to our table.

"Ah, Hanbresino," Rick exclaimed. Obviously, they had met before. "Meet my friends," Rick continued, "Everyone, this is Hanbresino Agusto." And he proceeded to introduce everyone to Hanbresino, who continued to stand while Rick kept talking.

"Pull up a chair," Stephen said. "At this table there's always room for one more."

"Ah, yes, of course," Rick said.

No one objecting, Hanbresino retrieved a chair from another table and sat down.

"Just order anything you want," Rick said, "on me."

Hanbresino proceeded to order a meal worthy of his name.

"Hanbresino is going to show us the interesting side of town," Rick said.

"I will take you to something you have never seen before," Hanbresino boasted.

"And what might that be?" Martin asked.

"A cockfight, just down the road, not too far."

"Sounds great," Margaret said.

"I don't know," Claudia said.

"No ladies," Hanbresino said. "It is not customary."

Claudia looked relieved.

"That's not right," Margaret said.

Hanbresino was adamant.

"I'd rather go shopping," Claudia said.

"It's not a good idea to buck local custom," Martin pontificated.

"All right," Margaret said. "I wouldn't want to irreparably damage local culture, if that's what you want to call this barbaric pastime."

"I don't call it anything," Martin said.

"All right, it's settled, Claudia and I will go shopping."

"Well, in that case, I'll stay with the ladies," Stephen said.

"Let's go then," Rick said.

"Not yet señores; cockfight's not till three o'clock."

"I don't think I want to go to a cockfight anyway," I said.

"Don't be hasty. We have time yet to decide," Martin said. "It may prove interesting."

Hanbresino had some errands to attend to, but he promised to return on time. True to his word, he showed up at half past two. The women had taken Stephen off to explore the downtown shops.

"How far is this place?" I asked, looking for a possible way out.

"Not too far," Hanbresino said. "Maybe twenty minutes to get there."

"No sweat," Rick said. "Well, a little sweat, maybe," he added. "Let's go."

"What the hell," I said.

A passenger car took us to the outskirts of town; then we followed Hanbresino down a trail leading away from the road. We walked through a clump of trees that stood listless in the heat of the afternoon, then out across some fields that lay fallow.

"Over the next hill there will be houses," Hanbresino said.

"Houses I don't care about," Martin said. "What about the fighting birds?"

"The birds will be there too," Hanbresino said.

"I'm thirsty," I said.

"There is a well there too, very good water," Hanbresino said.

"I wouldn't advise drinking the water from a well," Martin said.

"The water is good," Hanbresino said, "but you can buy Pepsi-Cola and also beer. The water is free."

"Thank you very much," Martin said.

As Hanbresino had promised, from the top of the hill we spied several shacks, the largest demarcated as a general store by the Pepsi-Cola sign out front. We followed Hanbresino down to the place. Behind the general store a crowd of men gathered about a round enclosure of wooden slats. No action yet in the pit, the men discussed the relative merit of each of the birds that would be fighting. The handlers stayed close to their birds that in bright plumage stood imperiously in their wooden cages oblivious to their imprisonment.

"I will introduce you to Enrique Jimenez, the most celebrated bird handler in all of Sonora," Hanbresino said.

The most famous bird handler in all of Sonora, a diminutive old man who kept his distance from the crowd, squatted in the dust making scribbles in the sand with a twig, all the while a smile fixed on his face. He looked up but did not speak as Hanbresino led us to him. Although in a still position, the old man seemed full of energy. He resembled one of the birds, his wiry body about to spring like a coil.

"Don Jimenez, these are my three friends from the North," Hanbresino said in Spanish.

Don Jimenez did not get up. He did not say anything, but only chuckled as if Hanbresino had said something amusing. Martin, Rick and I looked at each other. I shrugged.

"He seems off his rocker," Martin said under his breath, not knowing whether Jimenez understood English.

"No señores that is not the case," Hanbresino said. "You must not make hasty judgment. Don Jimenez is the best."

"Sometimes to be the best you have to have a loose screw," Rick said.

"You don't understand, Señor, but you will. You will see."

"I'm still thirsty," I said.

"Okay, Pepsis all around," Martin said. "What about Don Jimenez, will he drink a Pepsi with us?"

"No, he drinks only water," Hanbresino said.

"He's used to it, I suppose," Martin said, and he went into the general store to get the drinks.

A fat man, perhaps the owner of the store, an entrepreneurial air about him, seemed to be in charge of the event. He announced that the proceedings were about to begin. He took out a little notebook from his breast pocket and read from it the names of the birds to be matched and that of their handlers, ten matches in all. Don Jimenez had birds in four of them. The announcement merely a formality since everyone there seemed already well informed and had been making wagers all along. The fat man seemed to be the main bookie, and he now called for last minute bets on the first match.

"The birds must be weighed," a thin young man petulantly demanded, and after a few moments several other men joined to support his demand.

"Of course the birds will be weighed. Compadres, that goes without saying. We run an orderly establishment," the fat man said.

Hanbresino had taken us back to Don Jimenez now affixing the spurs on one of his birds. The hollow part of the steel spurs fit over the cock's own natural spurs, which had been cut back to allow a proper fit. The round and smooth steel spurs came in various sizes. Don Jimenez preferred the short spurs, more deadly in close combat.

"Jesus, this is barbaric," I said. "Half of all these beautiful birds will die today."

"Everything dies, sooner or later," Don Jimenez spoke for the first time.

"Yes, but this is for nothing, for sport."

"And when you die, will you die for something?"

I had no intention of dying, so I had no answer to the question. The fat man called for the first two birds to be put into the pit. "I don't know if I can watch this," I said.

"I never knew you to be so squeamish," Martin observed.

I had no answer to that either, the anticipated gore was not what disturbed me. In fact, I was curious to find out what my own reaction would be to the violence. The two birds in the pit made a few sallies at each other, but produced no damage. They circled, each looking to give the opponent a deadly blow. Their crests and wattles removed to make them

lighter, they wove and bobbed their heads. Both birds of a dark variety, red, black and brown feathers predominated. Handsome and proud birds but the grand spectacle of their beauty and their pride was leading to their undoing. The battle heated up considerably, but the crowd seemed to be disappointed. Neither bird had a flamboyant style. Don Jimenez's however seemed to be getting the worst of the fight, which did not bode well for Hanbresino who had placed a bet on that bird.

"Well, you can't win them all," Rick said to the boy patting him on the shoulder.

"Do not worry señores, the fight is not over," he replied.

"Hope springs eternal," Martin said.

The heretofore-hapless bird must have been heartened by those words, because it suddenly exhibited a surge of energy. It spread out its flight wings, which had been trimmed for the fight and made a leap over its opponent that, unable to duck fast enough, received a spur to its left eye. The blow, less than fatal but damaging, brought a cheer from the crowd. Hanbresino smiled as if to say he knew it all the time. The hurt cock on its side apparently unable to stand, Don Jimenez's bird decided to be sporting and refrained from pressing his advantage. The hurt bird's handler entered the pit.

"Will they stop the fight now?" I asked.

"No, it's to the death," Hanbresino said, annoyed at the mere suggestion that he might be robbed of a complete and decisive victory.

The handler set the injured bird on its feet with his good eye in position to see the enemy, who, like a true warrior incensed at the sight of blood, resumed the attack with double vigor. The injured cock had plenty of heart, and it did not give ground, but its wound kept it from gaining advantage. Both cocks tiring, Don Jimenez's bird now made another flying attack on his opponent's blind side. This time the spur cleaved the head. The fight over, Hanbresino went off to collect his winnings.

"This is too brutal for me," I said.

"It is kind of barbaric," Rick said, "but after all, civilization is only a mere patina on all of us. We're a lot happier when we face that fact."

"You're so god damn smug; you're insufferable," Martin said.

Rick had not expected Martin's outburst. "Maybe you're right," Rick said.

"I've had enough," I said. "I'm going back."

"I'll go with you," Martin offered.

"You don't have to," I answered.

"Are you sure?"

"I know my way," I said.

"Are you sure?" Rick echoed.

But I had already commenced my retreat and didn't bother to answer.

At the Shamrock

AFTER ASTRONOMY CLASS, Mario headed back to the South Campus.

"Hey! Mario old man, how are you?" It was Sam Bauer hailing him.

Mario had known Sam in junior high, but they had gone on to different high schools and had only recently discovered each other at the college.

"Let's go for a beer," Sam said.

Mario's first impulse was to decline. He found Sam's company distasteful. Sam was sort of a madman. His mouth seemed always on the verge of an epileptic convulsion. Yet behind the wild eyes, Mario discerned the wreck of a nice human being. Mario found himself walking down Amsterdam Avenue to the Shamrock Bar on 129th Street.

"You hate my guts, don't you?" Sam unexpectedly said.

Though taken aback by the statement, Mario remained composed. Distaste was not the same as hate, even if he had failed to sufficiently disguise his aversion to his companion. "No, certainly not, what do you mean?" he managed to stammer all the while wishing he had refused the excursion to the pub.

"You put me in the same category with the rest of them—with Norman and Marvin and them. I know you do."

"What makes you think that I disliked them?"

"How could you not? They're real pigs."

"It was a long time ago. We were children then. What does it matter now?"

"Childhood is an important time. Do you know that one's whole character is determined by the age of five?"

Mario remained silent as if he were considering the implications of that fact. If indeed it was a fact, it seemed an irrelevant one. He saw no need to reply.

"You can hate me if you want. I deserve it," Sam said.

The Shamrock Bar on Amsterdam Avenue was the only remaining White bar in the neighborhood. A few students wandered in now and then, but it was mostly patronized by White working class men who lived between the college and the Hudson. The Ballad of the Green Berets was playing on the jukebox. Sam and Mario ordered beer and sat at a booth.

"You have to admit they were real pigs. Right? I mean you can say it now."

Mario's resentment of his junior high classmates had taken a while to surface. But still, he mistrusted Sam's confirmation. "They were your friends," Mario said. "Why are you so down on them now?"

"Friends? Do you really think they were my friends? Do you really think that?"

"That's what I remember," Mario said. He remembered more. He had never hated Sam the way he hated the others. Sam had some redeeming quality—his madness perhaps. Sam had been a sort of holy fool, though he was far from stupid; on the contrary, he was rather brilliant and yet he played the buffoon, the victim. He was the one the tough boys picked on for fun. They loved to see him cringe and beg for mercy. Sam's lack of dignity and pride embarrassed

Mario as he had watched Sam give in to fear that the toughies would carry out their threats. Had Sam merely stood up to them they would have ceased to persecute him. Mario was certain that the bullies were only interested in the spectacle of Sam's groveling.

"Stand up to them, man. Stand up to them!" Mario had shouted in exasperation.

"They'll hurt me."

"Nonsense, they're just having fun with you because you let them."

"I don't want to get hurt! I don't want to get hurt!"

Mario was baffled. Wasn't there something more important than physical safety? How could anyone live without pride?

"You're not afraid of them, because they're Puerto Ricans, like you," Sam blurted.

Mario wanted to get rid of the implication of complicity, but there was no way to escape the feeling of shared responsibility for the violence, though it was no more sinister than the psychological violence that Sam's friends engaged in. Their venom was rarely directed at Mario, but the fear emerged nevertheless and transformed into enmity.

After they ordered their second beer at the Shamrock, Sam brought the conversation around to civil rights and the plight of Blacks, though he was neither poor nor Black. He punctuated every statement with the question, "Don't you agree?" Rhetorical of course, he rarely waited for a response. "If a Black man demanded my seat in the subway, I would get up and let him sit. He's entitled to it," he proclaimed.

"And what would that achieve?" Mario asked.

"Only justice," Sam answered. "Don't you believe in justice?" he asked in an accusatory tone. "Black women are beautiful," Sam declared abruptly, switching the focus of the conversation. "Don't you think so? Black women are the most beautiful women in the world. They're more beautiful than White women. I would never love a White woman. I would feel disgust to make love to a White woman. Tell me, don't you think Black women are superior?"

"Black or White doesn't make any difference to me when it comes to women," Mario said.

"No sir," Sam replied, "Black women are incomparable."

Mario kept quiet. Sam continued to rant about the superiority of Black women. Mario wondered whether his companion kept company with Black people at all.

"I have a Black girlfriend," Sam said. "She's wonderful."

Mario gulped down the last of his beer. "What about Claudia?" he wanted to say. Claudia, a member of the poetry workshop class, had revealed to the group that she had had a fling with Sam, but she had failed to tell him that she was married. He had assumed that she was an undergraduate like the rest of that group but she was really a graduate student hanging out with younger folk. Mario stifled the question, and instead said, "I'm heading back to campus."

"Get yourself a Black woman," Sam said. "It'll do wonders for you."

"Thanks," Mario said and got up to leave.

"I'm having another beer," Sam said.

"See you around."

Once outside, Mario looked back and saw Sam walk up to one of the regulars at the bar. "He's going to get hurt," Mario said to himself, then turned and headed back to Finley Hall.

Chickens' Tale

RETURNING TO THE HOTEL, Claudia and I came upon Don Gregorio, his English more fluid than I had surmised, narrating to Martin, who in turn quietly and uncharacteristically listened to the story of Pedro Humacao.

Don Gregorio claimed that Pedro Humacao had been a rare personage, indeed the sort of man encountered in literature or mythology, but rarely in the flesh, though Don Gregorio assured us, more than once, that Pedro Humacao had been a true and honest person whom he had personally known, and the veracity of whose exploits he was willing to vouch for. Don Gregorio's earnestness in this matter surprised me. My first impression of him dissipated, and he now had the look of a grocer who would keep his thumb on the scale when weighing something for a customer.

"*Era una época terrible y extraordinaria,*" he said turning to me. "But extraordinary times breed extraordinary men. Or rather ordinary men find themselves called to behave in most unusual ways. Had it not been a time of turmoil and revolution who is to say that Don Pedro would not have been just another *campesino* tilling his fields, had there been any fields to till around here." He chuckled after that last remark as if it had been an exemplary witticism.

"Well? And what was he like, this Pedro Humacao?" Martin asked, making a sly face, of uncertain meaning. I couldn't tell whether he knew quite well that we were about to be treated to a tall tale to be taken with a grain of salt, or whether he was pointing out another instance of authentic lore for savvy travelers to appreciate.

Don Gregorio continued in the most serious vein. "A simple man, but sometimes not very prudent. His will strong, he thought in his own way about many things, disregarding at his own peril, as he found out, the common wisdom that had been accumulated by his people over thousands of years. I say his people because he was an Indian and I am not, as you may have already guessed." Another of his witticisms, I noted.

"He got into a feud with a *brujo*. You know what that is, no, a medicine man, a man of power. Now this quarrel resulted from something insignificant, so insignificant that no one remembers for sure what it was, who knows, an imaginary affront, but Don Pedro took it to heart. His honor at stake, he would not listen to reason. His wife frantically begged him to drop the matter, to apologize to Don Paco, the *brujo*. But there was no moving Don Pedro. He did not believe in mumbo-jumbo, and if Don Paco could come up with any magic, it could not be anything Don Pedro himself could not also perform. Of course, everyone thought him quite out of his senses. His mother, an old woman, walked all the way from Cuernavaca, to try to dissuade him, her effort to no avail. If you had only seen the tears of that old woman! They could have melted a stone, but they did not move him.

"And you did see them?"

"In truth? No, I did not, but I heard a firsthand account of the matter as told to my mother by Don Pedro's sister-in-law."

"I see," Martin skeptically commented.

"Don Pedro kept a few chickens," Don Gregorio continued, "as many people do, and all of a sudden his chickens began to die. One by one they were found dead in the yard with no sign of external injury. Don Paco's doing, no doubt about it. Still, Don Pedro was not convinced, so he took one of the chickens to Dr. Gutierrez, at that time the only veterinarian in these parts. Dr. Gutierrez cut up the chicken and examined it, just like doing an autopsy in a murder investigation. He found nothing wrong with the chicken."

"Other than it was dead," I said.

"Yes of course, other than it was dead. But he found no sign of foul play or disease. The chicken just died without apparent cause. To everyone that was obviously ridiculous. You must agree that that is not an acceptable conclusion. One chicken one can ignore, but ten causes wonder. But one had not far to go in search of an explanation, everyone certain of Don Paco's involvement.

"Don Paco did not claim responsibility, but neither did he deny it. Of course, that was part of his method. Many unexplainable events were ascribed to the machinations of Don Paco only to be discovered, sometimes years later, that he had nothing to do with the matter. But at the time of the chicken incident everyone ascribed responsibility to Don Paco. The imagination of his neighbors supplied him with more power than he could ever hope to acquire by any other means, so he went along letting them think whatever they wanted.

"And though not particularly eager to arouse Don Pedro's ire, neither did he rush to quell the rumor. Perhaps he did not count on Don Pedro being so pigheaded. Anyone else would have found a way to mend things with Don Paco, regardless of who was at fault, the prudent course of action to prevent further unexplainable misfortune. Don Pedro, however, decided to take the bit in his teeth, or in other words, take the bull by the horns. He gave Don Paco an ultimatum: 'Restore the chickens in three days or else.' What he meant by the 'or else' not quite clear. At that point, all who knew him ceased to consider him rational and, that being the case, the possibility of violence loomed.

"Don Pedro had not the power of the occult with which to confront Don Paco on an equal footing. No one could guess what he had in mind; for if he intended to exact retribution, by common wisdom, he should have tried to catch the wizard by surprise instead of a head-on confrontation. Well, the three days went by and of course Don Pedro did not have his chickens back, the expected outcome. After all, one cannot bring chickens back from the dead any more than one can bring men."

"Well, Don Gregorio, don't you think he expected his chickens to be replaced, not brought back to life?"

"Quite so, quite so, but let's remember that we're dealing here with a *brujo* and a situation that already smacked of the supernatural. No one would have thought it beyond belief had the same chickens come back to life with the exception, of course, of the one that had been dissected by Dr. Gutierrez. The restoration of that one, everyone agreed, would require divine intervention, and it would be blasphemous to think that God would concern himself with such an inconsequential matter."

"So, what happened at the end of three days?"

"Listen to this," he said leaning forward and lowering his voice as if there were an interdiction against mentioning what he was about to relate, and he was risking limbs and life in revealing the outcome. "More dead chickens," he said in a whisper that came out more like a hiss.

"But," I protested, "I thought all of Don Pedro's chickens were already dead."

"Ah, yes, but these were Don Paco's chickens. Well, you can imagine the anxiety that rippled through the neighborhood. No one had ever before dared to cross Don Paco so directly without suffering dreadful consequences. I haven't told you the strangest part yet, which is this: Don Pedro claimed to be as surprised as everyone else. He insisted that he had nothing to do with the demise of Don Paco's chickens, though, at this point who could believe him? These chickens seemed to have died in the same manner as the first batch, no physical evidence of foul play. Don Paco not to be outdone by Don Pedro took one of his chickens to Dr. Gutierrez, the vet, who proceeded to cut this one open also, but not before proclaiming this to be the last time he would be involved in this quarrel in any way, for this cutting up of dead animals was of dubious value to his reputation, as he was not a butcher but a doctor. So he cut up Don Paco's chicken with the same results, no sign of an unnatural cause of death. The kicker, of course one might say, an indication of a supernatural agent at work. Who would have thought Don Pedro to have such resources at his disposal? This added a further mystery to the situation. Either Don Pedro had enlisted the aid of another *brujo* or he was a *brujo* himself. Either one of these explanations would have entailed a great deal of secrecy on Don Pedro's part. No one doubted that Don Pedro could keep a secret if he so wished, but this would have required that his family be quiet also, a wonder in itself.

"The neighborhood braced itself for trouble, or more accurately, it waited for Don Paco and Don Pedro to trounce each other, though most people still expected Don Paco to be the one dishing it out. There are, of course, in any community those who will always play the long shot. The gamblers put their money on Don Pedro. But no one expected what actually happened."

He paused and with seemingly vacant eyes looked across the courtyard, giving us a chance to digest the story. After a few moments we were ready for Don Gregorio to resume his narrative, but he continued to look around as if he had forgotten the story.

"What did happen?" I queried by way of urging him on.

Don Gregorio's lips curled up into an unnatural smile and an uncharacteristic cackle escaped from his throat, "Every chicken in the vicinity dropped dead, every single one, just like the others." Those words were followed by a long silence while Don Gregorio gazed at some distant imaginary object.

At the Country House

"It's wonderful to have a place you can always go to get away," Brian said. "It's good to have money as long as you don't become a slave to it. I know how to enjoy money. The rest of my family doesn't. They're always worrying about it. Me, I just enjoy it. That's the way to be. Don't you think so, Mario?"

"I guess so," Mario said.

In his VW, Brian was driving some of his fellow students up to his family's county house, a two-hour ride from the city. Nancy sat up-front next to him.

Mario rode in the back seat with Margaret. Not too long before, while sitting on the parapet in front of the Morris Cohen Library, she had been very forthcoming. Wearing a very short skirt that exposed a good portion of her thighs, she had beckoned him when she saw him walking toward 135th Street. As he approached her, he tried to keep his eyes on her face though the lower part of her body was difficult to ignore. Her smile, an automatic reflex, resembled a permanent injury incurred in an accident. She seemed to be trying to disguise a painful emotion. Her features projected an attractive but weathered appearance making her look older than her years. Her very short haircut, just coming into fashion, still looked very odd on a woman. They greeted each other, and she confessed to a splitting headache. She was waiting there for Rick.

"I just left him in the cafeteria," Mario informed her.

"Maybe he forgot he was supposed to meet me here," she said. "We were going to discuss this problem I have. You want to hear it?"

"Shoot," Mario said.

"Are you sure?" she asked. "I don't want to burden you with my problems. I hate people who do that, you know, always talking about how depressed they are. They depress everybody else."

"Don't worry, depression is not my thing," he said.

"Well, you see, out West this summer I met someone. I went down to Mexico, and then I traveled up the West Coast to Oregon. I met Bob in Mexico, but he's from Oregon, so I went there with him. He said he would marry me, and now he's coming to New York to see me. I wrote to him and told him not to come. I changed my mind about getting married. I don't even love him. Now I'm in love with Rick. But Bob wrote back saying he would come anyway."

"That's really a problem," Mario said. He sat down next her, and as she looked straight ahead scrutinizing the library facade, Mario's eyes insisted on roaming over her body and down to her thighs.

"Rick says he left his wife for me. I didn't ask him to do that. Now I feel terrible," she said. "It's not my fault, is it? I didn't ask him leave her."

"Nah, it's not your fault," Mario said. "You're just his excuse. He wouldn't have left her if he didn't want to anyway."

Mario tried to reassure her although he didn't think she was completely blameless. He saw no advantage in revealing what he really thought, so he concealed his perplexity about the matter. That day, he had left Margaret on the parapet the same way he had found her. Perhaps a little more at ease about the demise of a marriage, but he didn't think the mood would last. She wanted to feel blameworthy. Perhaps he had ingratiated himself a little more with her, but he saw no foreseeable dividend in that. She was physically attractive, but he otherwise found her dull. She affected being a scatterbrain, and sometimes she convinced herself. In any case, as long as she and Rick still had something going, he wasn't going to touch her. Now she was sitting next to him in the back seat of Brian's VW.

Looking at the autumn foliage as it flitted by, Mario paid scarce attention to what the others were saying. He'd heard it before. He remained uncertain of what his own attitude would be in the unlikely event of acquiring a great deal of money, or to be more accurate, on his coming by it, because he didn't contemplate acquiring it. Acquiring implied a calculated pursuit, and he had eliminated money from the goals to which he would apply pursuit. He didn't know exactly when he had made that decision. He had made it a long time before, in childhood—or he had started the process then, the decision having to be made repeatedly, over and over until it became irreversible. He didn't want to think about the matter now as he sat in the car riding to the country house of his friend's family. Brian treated his family's wealth as a glass eye, with a polite pretense that it was natural.

"I wouldn't dedicate my life to getting money," Brian said. "That's not my thing, but for some people that's what they enjoy. And that's all right, the game of it, you know? When it stops being a game, that's when it gets bad."

"Yeah, I guess so," Mario said.

"I think I would agree with that," Margaret put in.

"Everyone is so agreeable. How wonderful!" Nancy chimed. She was in a good mood sitting up front with Brian.

"Are you being sarcastic?"

"No, I mean it, really. I'm so happy. Are we almost there?"

"Almost," Brian assured her.

Dark by the time they arrived, the house downhill from the driveway, Brian went ahead to turn on the lights.

"Well, make yourselves at home," he said. The fatuous tone of his voice became more pronounced. "I think a fire is in order."

"Yes, it's chilly in here. I could go for some coffee," Nancy said.

"The kitchen is that way," Brian said as he pointed.

He stacked some wood in the fireplace and tried to light it, but the fire wouldn't start.

"These fucking logs are too big. We're going to have to split them."

"Oh, I'm good at that," Margaret said.

"Are you?" Brian smirked as he looked up at her. "This is man's work."

"Oh, come on, I want to try," she said.

"It's okay with me, if it's okay with Mario."

"It's all right with me. I'm just going to sit here and pretend the fire is already roaring."

Margaret and Brian went outside to split the logs. Mario listened for the sound of the axe striking the wood, but it didn't come.

"Is this the way?" he heard Margaret ask.

"Yeah, that's perfect," Brian answered.

Nancy came back from the kitchen.

"Where's everyone?"

"Everyone is out splitting wood," he said. After a short pause, he added, "Anyway, that's what they said they were going to do."

"What do you mean by that?"

"I don't hear the axe."

Red blotches spotted Nancy's face. The corner of her eyes became moist.

"What do you think they're doing out there?"

"I don't know," he said. "They're not splitting wood."

"If you think they're doing something out there, why don't you come right out and say it?" she snapped at him simultaneously trying to repress anxiety.

Mario picked himself up from his sprawl on the couch. Nancy disgusted him at the moment—her weakness, her blindness, her lack of dignity, her frail appearance, the sickly quiver of her lips. He wanted to shout at her, "They're feeling each other up. That's what they're doing. And do you know what Brian really thinks of you? He thinks you're the silliest, sorriest woman he's ever met." Unable to react, he kept quiet. He didn't think enough of her to get worked up; perhaps he merely pitied her and saw no reason to hurt her further.

She'd been confiding in him during the past few weeks. She thought herself in love with Brian; sure that he desired her. He had tried to warn her tactfully without betraying Brian's confidence, but she wouldn't listen. She embraced her fantasy, and Brian enjoyed exploiting it.

"She thinks you're in love with her," Mario had said to Brian. "I'm sure she doesn't think that," Brian replied with obvious delight. "Why would she think that? It's a preposterous notion." Not anyone's guardian, Mario had retreated to his post of observer.

"Don't be angry at me," he lashed back at Nancy. "Whatever they do is not my business."

"There's the axe. I hear it now."

"I hear it too," he said.

"They're just splitting wood. You shouldn't imply things about people."

"No, I shouldn't," he said.

Margaret and Brian came back into the house, Margaret's face flushed, Brian carrying the wood.

"This sure is hard work," she said.

Nancy scrutinized Margaret's face and then went back to the kitchen to check on the coffee. The fire going, they all sat by the fireplace. Nancy sat next to Brian on the couch.

"I wonder what Rick is doing right now?" Nancy said. "I wish he had come."

"I invited him," Brian said.

"Rick can be such a drag sometimes," Margaret said.

"He's nice, but when he goes into one of his moods, he's hard to take. And he gets into them so often."

"He's morose," Brian said. "Moroseness has to be done away with."

"Still, I think he's a fine person, and he loves you, Margaret. When a man is in love with me, I try to understand him," Nancy pontificated.

"Let's not talk about love," Margaret suggested. "Let's talk about something more cheerful."

"I heard Sam Bauer got thrown down a flight of stairs," Mario said.

A burst of laughter emanated from Brian. Nancy tried to make herself smaller and blend into the couch.

"Thrown, did you say?" Brian asked in between guffaws. "Who threw him?"

"I don't know," Mario said. "I was wondering whether any of you knew more about it."

"Do you know anything, Nancy?" Margaret asked not missing a chance at getting her licks.

Nancy, for a moment uncertain of what stance to take, decided to laugh it off. "It was Jay," she said. "Sam came to the house to see me, and Jay threw him down the stairs."

She had told Sam that Jay, her husband, was her brother. Jay didn't really mind her having a lover, but he nevertheless found Sam obnoxious. Brian laughed even more on hearing this explanation. In contrast to his stocky body, he had a thin high-pitched laughter.

"I think we're ready for some of this stuff," Brian said as he pulled out a little pouch. "I was keeping this a secret to surprise you all." From the pocket of his shirt he produced a small red and blue box of cigarette paper. He proceeded to roll a joint, and after taking the first drag he passed it to Mario, who wondered why Brian hadn't passed it to Margaret or Nancy first, but what the hell, that was Brian. The mood set for the evening, from then on everyone giggled at the slightest prompt. Brian brought out a copy of *Portrait of the Artist as a Young Dog*, and between fits of laughter they took turns reading.

After the uncontrolled mirth had exhausted them, Brian said, "We have to divvy up the beds."

The house had three bedrooms. The one with two beds, Brian shared with his brother when his whole family came up to the country. The attic served as the guest bedroom. The two women were to sleep in the bedroom that had the two beds, and Mario in the attic. Brian decided to sleep in the living room.

"Why don't you sleep in the master bedroom?" Margaret asked.

"That's my parent's bed. I don't ever sleep there."

"They wouldn't know," she said.

"I'd know," he rejoined.

Next morning the mood was less than cheerful. Three of them sat at the breakfast table.

"Where's Nancy?" Brian asked after breakfast. Nancy had yet to join them.

"I think she went for a walk," Mario said.

"I don't think she should be by herself," Margaret said. "Why did you let her go?"

"I'm not her keeper," Mario said.

"We better find her."

"I'll look down by the lake," Mario said. "I've been meaning to take a walk down there anyway."

"Let's search by the road," Brian suggested to Margaret.

No boats on the water at the moment, the dark water of the lake stretched calmly for miles. Trying to figure out which way Nancy might have gone, Mario slowly walked down to the dock. He stood for a while listening to the water lap against the pier. Around the lake, the trees had burst into yellow, orange, and purple hues. Shortly, he spied Nancy perched on a on a log near the water. Posing for the search party, she sat looking into the distance, her knees tucked under her chin. As he approached, she turned and gasped in studied surprise. Her face displayed the disappointment that Mario, and not Brian, had found her.

"We've been worried about you," he said.

"I'll bet they've been worried. I'll bet! How could they do this to me? The two of them, I thought they were my friends."

"They're not doing anything," he said, trying to keep her calm, although he had been up early and hearing voices downstairs had looked down from the attic to see Margaret and Brian on the couch together.

"She must have thought I was still sleeping, but I heard her get up," Nancy said.

"Did you?" he said rather than asked.

"I've been thinking that I could jump into this lake and drown myself."

Tired of her melodramatic stances, he tried to maintain some concern in his voice. "That's a little drastic, don't you think?"

"I was going to jump in, but then I thought, 'They're not worth it.'"

"You're right about that," he said.

She sulked the rest of the day and all the way back to the city. A few days later, Mario heard that Rick had given Margaret her walking papers.

A Valley of Tears

ENRIQUE FELT CONSPICUOUS as he walked from his car to his mother's place. As usual, he had not been able to find a spot on the same block. She lived close to a shopping street that drew much traffic. He was not averse to walking, but he would have preferred a spot closer to the building because he did not like to prolong the sense of being out of place. Although he had grown up on these streets, he could not escape the feeling that he was in a foreign country whose customs though familiar, were alien, and though he spoke the language he would never be able to make himself fully understood.

He could not pinpoint the time when the sidewalks in disrepair became noticeable, when the grass spilling over from an empty lot and growing through the cracks in the broken slabs became as disturbing as the rampant litter and the unheeded garbage. Those conditions had once been for him the norm, not to be noticed because they were always there. He went past the *bodegas* where groups of men sat in their undershirts drinking beer and playing dominoes. He could not understand how they could play that game for hours as if there were nothing in the world more satisfying. There was something marvelous about it, a quaint simplicity he reluctantly admired. He looked at them as he imagined Adam might have looked back at the Garden, with longing and with the fear that he might be recognized as one who had been cast out.

Long ago he had abandoned these streets. He had slowly grown away from them, though while it was happening he had thought that it was he who was being abandoned. Now he was not sure. Perhaps it was both. He was often faced with the conundrum of whether he had a choice, of whether circumstances dictated his choices, and if so, were they choices at all? Are we managed by fate the way we manage a child when we say "Do you want to drink your milk sitting in this chair or that chair?" and so involved in choosing between chairs, he does not consider that he might want to stand or run or jump. It may be that if we had enough information about the past, we would be able to foretell the future. What then is free will but an illusion created by our ignorance? This was a logical enough conclusion, but one difficult to accept.

He saw that many of the psychological discomforts of life stemmed from the inability to reconcile conflicting truths and perceptions, for all truths are necessarily consistent, and he had to fall back on his ignorance to account for disparities. Enrique rued the fact that he was not ignorant enough to have remained in a state of bliss, that as a mortal he was condemned to never arrive at the other side, never attain knowledge equivalent to a state of grace. He had no hope of attaining it, nor did he wish to, through the conventional means of religion. To him faith was no substitute for knowledge, though he saw the value of that quality possessed by the truly religious, and also by the truly mad, of simultaneously believing in contradictory ideas. Such states are, after all, natural in some part of the mind. In dreams, a person may be in two places at the same time, simultaneously dead and alive. Often in the past, those who could bridge the gap between the physical world and the dream world were looked upon as holy people, saints. At present, however, Joan of Arc would merely be considered a deranged person in need of medical care. He recalled seeing a painting of Joan of Arc in a textbook as an illustration of a disease of which hallucinations are a common symptom. With this advance in knowledge how many great exploits have been prevented; how many saints have gone undiscovered?

Invariably, when he visited his mother, his mind turned to religion. It was both a bond and a rift between them. The discarded religious education of her son was one of the many disappointments of her life. It was not in her nature, however, to despair, and she did not give up hope that he would eventually return to the fold. She would often say to him, "I never stop praying to the Lord for your return to the Church. You were so devout when you were a little boy, and you will be again someday. God will hear my prayers."

He never took her words as chiding nor her prayers as reproaches. "I haven't strayed as far as you think," he said to allay her fears. He thought it beyond her understanding to grasp how far he had reached on a course from which there was no turning back.

He did not know what he would say to her today to calm fears, for today they were not about his relation to the Church. That was an old concern that had started when he was younger. They had now grown accustomed to each other's position, and though they were each aware of the issue, they were content to leave it in the background. She had summoned him to discuss something, if not more urgent, at least more immediate. This time he did not have reason on his side.

He reminded himself that he was an adult. He did not have to answer to his mother the way he did as a child, but the surroundings conspired against him. The smells from the cooking going on in the various apartments pervaded the stairwell. It reminded him of the days when he had run up and down the stairs to do errands, to take out garbage, or just to play with the other children. He had thought that he had left all that behind, and he was now surprised at how it all easily came back threatening to overwhelm him.

The necessity to ring the doorbell at the moment reprieved him, and as he focused his total attention on pressing the button his panic subsided. He waited to hear the footsteps on the other side, a familiar and comforting activity when facing that door. He recalled as a child learning to distinguish whose footsteps they were merely by the sound. That accomplishment had been a source of pleasure.

Enrique kissed his mother on the cheek and followed her down the long corridor past the bedrooms on the right, one she kept for guests, anyone in need who applied to her for a temporary place to stay, then past her own, with the big bed on which she had slept alone now for many years. At the end of the corridor, they entered a small foyer, to the right the bathroom and the kitchen, to the left, the dining room and the living room. Through the windows, light flooded the living room. It was unusual for the two of them to be there alone. They saw each other mostly when the whole family gathered, but this time she had asked to see him alone.

She did not often request anything of him, and he did not refuse her anything that did not conflict with his convictions. This time, he dreaded the encounter because he expected her to ask for an explanation, and he had no comfortable one to offer. He had looked in a mirror once and had been startled by the image of his father looking back at him. It had been an discomforting experience, but he had calmed himself with the thought that the resemblance was only physical. He was afraid now that his mother would hold up a different kind of mirror, and he would see another resemblance to his father that he would not be able to brush aside so easily.

Doña Ramona brought out coffee, and she put the two cups on the dining room table. Before sitting down, she remembered that he was fond of tea biscuits, and she went back to the kitchen to fetch them. On returning she sat down. The coffee comforted him as he waited for her to bring up the subject she wanted to discuss.

"I had a talk with Anna," Doña Ramona said.

"Ah," he said, as if to indicate that he understood all the ramifications of the statement, and he did not need to talk about it any further, but that he would if she insisted. He knew that to get away with so simple a statement was too much to expect.

She was not in a hurry. She sat a few moments without saying anything as if his one word was a pictogram from the *I Ching* and she was contemplating all its possible meanings. If she found his response insufficient, she did not reveal it.

"She's not happy," Doña Ramona said.

"No, she's not happy," Enrique echoed.

It seemed to him that the understated remark had a

physical effect on the room, consuming the available oxygen faster than it could be replenished, and soon there would not be enough for him to breathe. He looked for signs of similar distress in his mother, but he detected none. There was no question that she had more fortitude than he, but he had not imagined that he would be put to a test.

"The earth is a valley of tears," he said in response to her remark about Anna. He wasn't sure whether he was trying to elicit sympathy by choosing a tenet of the Church or whether he was merely being facetious.

"Tears of our own making," she said.

There was no way for him to take that but as a reproach.

"Do you think I set out to make her unhappy?"

"Only you and God know that," she said.

He would prefer to leave God out of it, but he knew that she would not, that she could not.

"You want to tell me what's going on?" she continued.

"I wish I knew," he said.

"You must know something," she said. "Everyone else does."

"I know everything is out of control," he said.

"You expected control," she said. It was not a question.

He looked straight into her soft eyes, and he realized that it was statement of surprise. She had expected more from him.

"I can't say that I consciously had expectations," he said. "I didn't expect Anna to be unhappy."

"You expected her to turn a blind eye?"

"I didn't intend for her to find out is what I mean."

"That's expecting control," she said.

"And you think that's unreasonable?"

"I don't know," she said, "Are impossible and unreasonable the same things?"

He had not expected her to take that tack, and he was confused and embarrassed. He felt himself slipping into a childish mode. He blurted what first came to mind, "Are you angry at me?"

"No," she said, "I'm only sad. I thought you would escape this curse. I don't know why I thought that. It's in the blood. I thought the same about your father. I thought he would be different, but I was mistaken."

"It's not the same," he said, "It's not the same at all."

It was her turn to respond with the enigmatic, "Ah."

"It's completely different," he repeated.

"You don't want to divorce Anna?"

"Of course I don't," he blurted before carefully weighing his answer.

He had previously decided not to lie to his mother, and now he was not sure that he was keeping to his resolve. But perhaps his unconsidered answer was the best gauge of the truth. It was at least spontaneous, uncontaminated by thought, and that's what, in most instances, he trusted to be his genuine feelings. But spontaneous reactions that emanated from fear were often regrettable, and at the moment, he was uncertain whether he was acting out of fear of disapproval, or worse yet, out of fear that he was lurching uncontrollably towards resembling his father more than physically. His mother might be right, that it was in the blood; not literally, the way she meant it, but metaphorically, inevitably and beyond his control.

"I want to make it up to her," he said.

"How do you make up for something like that?" she asked.

He saw her point. He had meant to say that he wanted to make up with her, but the phrase had come out wrong, or perhaps it had come out right, because what he really needed to do to compensate was to show regret. And yet he saw that his mother was right. There was no way to retract what he had done. He understood that from all outward signs, though he did not truly feel remorse about a common transgression. That was the worst excuse in the world, but it was, after all, true.

"Your father was always trying to make it up to me," she said, "but he never did what would have done it. He never stopped, and that's what it takes."

"I know that," he said, because he thought that was what he should say. "I know what I have to do."

"Knowing what you have to do and doing it are two different things," she said.

"I don't want to lose Anna," he said, "but maybe it's too late."

"I don't think you can let yourself off the hook so easily," she said. "You can't put the blame on her, not without even trying to make it right."

"I don't know how I got into this predicament. Sometimes you stop to look around, and you have no idea where you are and how you got there. That's how I feel."

"You let go of your moorings, and you threw away your compass."

"Don't start in about the Church. That's not the issue.

I have to find my own way," he said. "Everyone can't go down the same road."

"You're right about that," she replied. "Same destination, different paths, I understand that."

He wondered whether she really did understand, whether she knew how different the paths were, or whether it was he who was deceived about the complexity of the situation. He found himself in the anomalous position of having his whole life reduced to just that, a situation, and perhaps one not as complex as he had imagined. It was not the elaborateness of the trappings that made for complexity.

That too, he knew well enough.

A Colorless Decision

IN MID-DECEMBER ARTURO was called for jury duty. In the central jury room, he met a woman who told him she would rather be home cooking. She was a short blond with wrinkles around her eyes and a frightened look, like a child in an unfamiliar place suddenly having the need to hold on to a parent's hand.

"In our Christmas celebration there are twelve dishes and some of them are very elaborate and take a great deal of preparation," she said in a very thick Eastern European accent.

Arturo nodded as if he knew what she was talking about. Perhaps she was referring to some Polish custom. He had nothing on which to base this assumption. He was merely guessing. She obviously wanted to talk, but at that moment he was satisfied with his guess.

"The last two days I got my husband to help," she said, almost chuckling, as if she had put something over on her husband.

"Yes, there's a lot to be done before Christmas," Arturo agreed. "My wife has been baking and freezing things. We're having a Christmas party on Sunday. We'll decorate the tree."

"Oh, you did that already. That's great."

"No," he explained, "we're doing it this coming Sunday. It's a tree trimming party."

"What a great idea," she said. "Do you use a real tree or an artificial one?"

"A real tree," he said.

"How do you get it to last?" she asked. "We got a real tree one year and in a few days the branches had all drooped."

"I just put sugar water in the base. Some people add an aspirin. I don't do that, but people say it works."

"Do you know what the fine is for not showing up for jury duty?" she asked, going back to what was on her mind.

"No, I don't," he said.

"It used to be two hundred dollars, but I don't know what it is now. I know a guy who just tore up the summons, and nothing happened to him. They didn't go after him."

Arturo saw in her eyes that she had seriously contemplated not showing up, and she was still wondering whether she had made the right decision. "They randomly choose who they're going to go after," he said. "It's too expensive to go after everyone." He didn't really know whether that was true or not, but he felt he should say something that didn't encourage breaking the law.

"I didn't see any restaurants around here," she said. "Do you suppose there are any?"

"Sure," he said, "if you walk down Cadman Plaza, a few blocks west you come to Montague Street. There're lots of restaurants on Montague."

"You seem to know downtown Brooklyn."

"I live nearby," he said. "And you?"

"Flushing," she answered.

"So you got here on the F train?"

"So you know your trains too. I have to take two buses

just to get to the subway. Then it's a walk from the subway to the courthouse, not an easy trip," she said.

Later, they were possible jurors for the same case, and she sat next to him again.

*

At the trial, the arresting officer, Henry Hogan, was called to the stand and took the oath.

"Will you please describe to the court how you came to arrest the defendant," the assistant district attorney, Mr. Stolley, said to the officer.

"On routine patrol of the park, I noticed the defendant and another person, a woman, sitting in a car smoking and passing the object back and forth, so my partner and I approached. I asked the defendant to step out. At first he refused, but at my insistence, he got out of the car. I asked him to turn around and put his hands on the car. He began to do so, but before completing the move, he bolted and ran towards the concession stand. As he ran, he kept his right hand at his waist. I followed him into the building. There was another man at the sink washing his hands. The defendant had entered one of the stalls. I ordered him to step out. I heard a metallic object hit the floor, and then the defendant came out. He attempted to walk by me, but I restrained him. By that time my partner had arrived at the scene. I looked in the stall and saw the gun on the floor."

"Did you subsequently check whether the gun is licensed to the defendant?"

"The serial number on the gun had been filed off."

"Thank you, Officer Hogan."

The defense attorney approached the witness stand.

"At any time, did you see the defendant holding the gun?"

"No, I did not."

"Were the defendant's fingerprints found on the gun?"

"No, they were not."

The prosecutor then called an FBI fingerprint expert to the stand.

"What is the general outcome of fingerprint analysis on hand guns?"

"The lack of fingerprints on such a weapon is usual. The gun surface is not conducive to retaining finger prints, so only in twenty-five percent of cases are they successfully retrieved."

That was all the available testimony, and the jury was sequestered for deliberation.

*

Five members of the jury were Black, five White, one Asian and one, Arturo, Hispanic. On the first ballot three voted for guilty, three for innocent and six undecided. On the second vote, seven went for guilty and five for innocent. All five votes for acquital came from Black jurors. Only one of the Black jurors was open to persuasion, but she was not going to change her vote as long as the other Blacks held firm.

"The facts of the case are clear," Arturo argued. "The verdict has to be guilty."

"I just want you all to know that race has nothing to do with my vote. The fact that I'm Black and he's Black is not a factor in my decision," one of the Black women said.

"Same with me," said another. "I would vote the same way if he were White."

Arturo was sure that they believed what they said at that moment, but he was also sure that it was not a true statement.

"The evidence is very strong," the youngest of the Black women said, "but it's only circumstantial. The gun was not actually seen in his hand. I can't take a chance of voting guilty if he's not."

Martha Stolley, the oldest of the three Black women, was short and stout, and throughout the proceedings she kept a severe and angry countenance. "The policeman was foolish to chase a man with a gun without waiting for backup or drawing his own weapon."

"Well, he didn't suspect the guy had a gun."

"He should have suspected when he saw the guy was running with his hand to his waist."

"Obviously this cop is not the brightest man in the world, but the evidence is clear, and it points to the guy having a gun. The cop didn't immediately think so; he had fixated on drugs, his mind ran along that one track, and he probably thought the defendant was only holding on to a greater stash than he had at first thought."

"But he should have known," she insisted. "He's trained to know these things."

"I was trained to do my job also, but how many times do I make mistakes and overlook things that I shouldn't? Granted that the cop was foolish in not suspecting a gun earlier, but that doesn't lessen the guilt of the defendant," Arturo argued.

"He had a bad attitude," she said about the defendant, "but that doesn't mean he had a gun."

The third woman on the jury focused on the other man who had been in the restroom when the cop arrived. This man

according to be policeman was standing by the washbasins washing his hands.

"Why couldn't it have been his gun?" she asked.

"Because the gun was in the stall from which the defendant emerged twelve feet away."

"Yes," said the man to the right of Arturo, a White juror, "why would that man have left the gun in the stall for no apparent reason."

"Maybe the defendant told him about the cop on his tail, so the man by the sink decided to get rid of the gun."

"There was not enough time for all that. He would have had to take out the gun slide it across the floor to the last stall, and resume washing his hands. That would have been too risky. If it was his gun, his best bet was to keep it hidden and walk out and disappear as he did. If the gun were his, he would have taken it with him."

"Well, it's a public restroom. A lot of people go there. Anybody could have left the gun there."

"In all the years that I have used public restrooms I never saw a gun in one of them. Have you?" Arturo asked.

"It's different in Brooklyn," she said.

"Yes, that sort of thing happens in Brooklyn," the one Black male juror said. His brother, his nephew and a cousin were policemen.

"I've lived in Brooklyn for twenty-five years," Arturo said. "I never saw a gun in a public restroom. Did any of you ever find a gun in a public restroom?"

No one had.

"Do you know anybody who found a gun a public restroom?"

Negative again, but all five insisted that was the sort of thing that happens in Brooklyn with some regularity.

"A gun like the one in evidence is an expensive item. It's worth a few hundred dollars. Why would anybody just leave it in a restroom unless, like the defendant, he was trying to avoid arrest?"

"No one saw him holding the gun, so it's possible that it's not his gun."

"It's possible, but not probable," Arturo said.

"I can't vote guilty unless I'm absolutely sure."

"Does that mean you're not willing to accept circumstantial evidence?"

"I suppose that's what it means."

"The charge from the judge was that circumstantial evidence must have the same weight as direct evidence."

"Be that as it may," she said, "my vote is not guilty."

That was that. There was no moving her from that position.

*

The young man to Arturo's right, Andrew Dossing, on the breaks, was reading the Wall Street Journal. After perusing the stock quotes he looked up and said, "I'm losing money every day."

"You're losing money in a surging market?"

"I had very bad picks this year," he said, as if annually he picked a whole new set of stocks.

"Look up Apogee," Arturo said. He sometimes traded that stock. He hadn't, however, held it for a while.

The young man looked it up. "It's 9½ up ¼," he said. "The high was 22 and the low 7."

"Yes, that's what it does. It fluctuates between 7 and 22," Arturo said. "I've been watching it for some years."

"It's a good buy, then, at 9½."

"Yes it is," Arturo said.

"How long have you been following it?"

"About five years," Arturo said, though really closer to ten.

"What do they make?" he asked.

"Glass for skyscraper windows and for cars."

He circled the stock in the paper. "I'll have to research this," the young man said.

On the second ballot Arturo voted guilty and stuck to it. To his right sat another young man, rather cheerful and outgoing. He had volunteered to be the foreman. He too voted guilty on the second ballot. On the third, he voted not guilty. He later explained that it was to see whether it would have any effect on the adamant ladies. He figured he could change his vote back to guilty if there was any possibility of getting a conviction. These two young men on Arturo's right were, like him, computer programmers. Another man on the jury had a happy face—thin with a twinkle in his eyes that revealed a quiet amusement. Always alert and smiling, he didn't do much talking. He wore an earring in his left ear, but he was not flamboyant or odd in any other way. He looked totally comfortable.

The line was drawn and everyone stuck to his or her vote, a hung jury. After the defendant was dismissed the judge asked the jurors to remain in the room for a discussion. He and the attorneys each spoke to the jurors, trying to reassure them that arriving at no consensus was alright, part of the system, and they shouldn't be disillusioned, it did indeed work. Arturo wanted to ask whether preventing social unrest was more important than upholding the law. But he kept his mouth shut and went home to think about it.

Justo Granudo

MANY PARISHIONERS LIVED on the mountainside, and Father Rodrigo, in the zealous performance of his apostolic duties, often traveled tending to his scattered flock. On this occasion, having been caught in a rainstorm, he was forced to spend the night away from town at the home of Lorenzo Palofuerte, a typical man of the parish. He worked for wages in the tobacco fields and cultivated his own land on which he grew vegetables for his household. He doted on his young wife, Maria, who had recently become a mother.

Lorenzo's father was also staying the night. The old man had eyes that twinkled constantly, as if he knew a joke no one else had heard. There was calmness behind the glitter. The priest was often intimidated by this merriment, by the sureness of it, a quality he longed for and was disappointed in not having found in the bosom of the church. The old man had a playful maliciousness against which the priest felt defenseless. Deep within, he resented that investiture had not provided him with a charm against the impishness of this old man.

"Witches were here last night, Father," said the old man. "They won't come back tonight though, with you here."

"Stop kidding," admonished Maria as she went around the table scooping rice into each plate. She was mockingly stern with her father-in-law. Although she felt constrained to respect the priestly garb of the younger man, she enjoyed arguments between the two.

"Maria burned the shit they left in the yard. Keeps them away. Gives them a terrible pain in the ass," the old man winked at Maria. She tossed her head slightly back suppressing a smile.

Father Rodrigo did not know whether to take the words humorously or, on behalf of the church, to take offence. He assumed a bland expression as he said, "That's preposterous."

"But it always works," Maria retorted with an urgency that revealed that the incident had in fact occurred.

"Witches do not exist," Father Rodrigo continued trying to weal authority, but his demeanor was a detriment. He was of slight build, and though his face was beginning to show the wear of thirty-seven years, there lingered a smidgen reminder of adolescence.

"Don't you believe in the devil, Father?" the old man facetiously asked.

"There are forces of evil."

"There you have it. It's this way: saints have direct contact with God, and witches with the devil. You can't believe in one without the other. Don't you sell medals in church, charms against meeting up with Satan?"

"To encounter the devil is a figure of speech. It doesn't mean you meet up with a flesh and blood creature."

"Of course it's not flesh and blood; it's a spirit."

"I think I saw my mother's spirit once," interjected Maria, adding a twist to the conversation.

"Did you?" asked the priest a little bewildered.

"It was right after her death," Maria went on, "during the vigil. I looked out the window, and there she was peering from behind the latrine."

The old man proceeded before the priest could recover. "Alfonso, who lived in the parish before you came, had a house about a mile up from here." The dim lighting from the kerosene lamp on the table accentuated the affected gravity of the old man. Every word was dramatic. "Once, as he was riding home, he was almost thrown from his horse. He quieted the animal and noticed a strong smell of magnolias though the flower grew nowhere near. He reached home to find that his wife had died. To his astonishment, by her side lay a bunch of magnolias."

"The front door shook hard when we were saying the rosary for her," said Lorenzo. "To this day we don't know whether someone was joking." He cut a piece of avocado, poured a little milk in his plate mashing the fruit in with the rice, and continued to eat in silence.

"Might have been Alejandra," Maria put in. "She's just the sort to do a thing like that. She's a little cracked, just the sort to go rattling doors in the middle of the night. Remember her, Father? She's in the woods all the time, collecting herbs just like a witch. It's not natural for an old woman to be living all alone in an out of the way place, as if she had no relatives. The other day she was hovering around here, trying to put the evil-eye on the baby."

The lack of headway in his campaign to eradicate superstition disturbed Father Rodrigo. When he had first arrived at Rio Alto he had been dismayed. The town was smaller than he had imagined. Situated on the side of a hill, the poorer section, shacks with roofs of tar paper or galvanized tin, looked as if it were about to slide down on the rest of the town. The church, at the bottom of the hill, seemed in a geologically precarious position which the priest translated into a spiritual one. Once the idea had entered his mind, he was on a constant lookout for sources of danger. He soon discovered that he was surrounded by popular superstitions, and he obsessively feared that his spiritual health was being assailed. His reaction to the parish folklore was so dominated by violent emotions that the parishioners considered that aspect of his character a quirk. What seemed peculiar was not that he disbelieved any one story—no story was believed by everyone—but that he flatly denied the possibility of the whole category of phenomena. He did not offer disproof, nor did he even show skeptical curiosity. He merely considered the existence of witches, spirits and demons an idea to be fought. But his method was too simple; it consisted only of vehement denial. At the root of his attitude lay a great fear, as if a hideous insect had already laid eggs in his soul; the larva had gnawed at it, and the chrysalis were waiting to spew forth the black winged ravagers as soon as he weakened. They would devour the living remnant. Then all that would be left would be the empty shell of his body in which the beating of innumerable black wings would be heard churning the putrid air. The image horrified him.

The next morning before his departure, Maria brought her baby for Father Rodrigo to bless. He knew that the mother had the evil eye in mind, and that she thought of this blessing as protection against it. Resignedly he blessed the child and departed. On his way home, the mortification caused by the previous evening was intensified by the condition of the road.

He had traveled but a short distance before his shoes were completely caked with mud. Occasionally, a breeze shaking the leaves above sprinkled him with an unwelcome baptism, so that as he made his way down the mountain, he became less than dry. From certain parts of the road, the town far below was visible. On bright days the sun beat down on the tin roofs making them sparkle, but the sunlight was at the moment obstructed by clouds; and Father Rodrigo, wet and troubled by the memory of the evil eye, was beset by the image of Christ on a mountain, prophesying the fall of Jerusalem.

Enthralled by these thoughts, he arrived at a ravine through which flowed a river spanned by a wooden bridge. The night's rain had caused the water to rise, and it was now flowing over the bridge. Some logs had been pried loose. His feet already wet, Father Rodrigo saw no reason to hesitate, and holding on to the railing, he began to cross. Looking into the turbulent and muddy water, which rushing by buffeted his ankles, he could not help but think of the demons that were reputed to live in the whirlpools of the river. Half way across he slipped, and as he grasped the rail with both hands, he caught sight of a figure behind him.

Father Rodrigo continued across, and when he reached the bank, a wolflike dog continually growling and showing its teeth confronted him. The stranger, of medium height and very sturdy appearance, his dark eyes accentuated by bushy brows, caught up and stepped between the priest and the dog. "I'm Justo Granudo," he said in an unexpectedly humble manner.

The two men proceeded along the same road. The dog, of which Father Rodrigo assumed Justo was the master, ragged and dirty, showed no sign of having reaped the benefits of domestication. Its following at Justo's heels was the only indication that it was a tamed animal. There was no visible leash, but the impression that man and beast were tugging at each other was inescapable. The animal's growl was constant—rich and awesome in its implications. A horror coupled to inexhaustible vigor, the sound elicited a fear of an unfathomable darkness so replete with life that excess had gone beyond the curious to become grotesque. Chaos lurked in that sound—jealous, resentful, desiring to reclaim a domain that had been stolen. Yet the priest was aware of resonant tones hinting at bright emptiness, like the light filled spaces of a cathedral.

The sun came out and shone through the leaves causing erratic patterns of light and shade. Father Rodrigo felt uneasy as he walked with the stranger. Conversation proved futile. Being asked where he came from, Justo Granudo made a gesture that the priest took to mean the other side of the ridge. Despite this taciturnity, and contributing to the discomfort, Father Rodrigo was convinced that silence was not habitual with Justo Granudo. Repeatedly the priest turned his head to gaze at his companion. For some reason he was unable to remember Justo's face, and had to continually check to make certain of its details. The thought that each time he looked he saw something different took root in the soil of his anxious imagination, and like lush vegetation in a tropical forest, began an uncontrollable growth. The priest began to suspect that this stranger might be some desperate sinner, the state of whose soul was the cause of the unpleasantness. He had nothing substantial on which to base this assumption, yet

the certainty that the stranger was a criminal was preferable to the possibility that he might be something else.

Suddenly, the dog leaped forward sinking its teeth into Justo Granudo's leg. Justo's face became contorted in pain as he uttered a long piercing shriek. Blood gushed from the wound. Father Rodrigo picked up a stick and tried to drive the animal away from the man, but no sooner had he stepped between the two that Justo Granudo burst out laughing. The laugh reverberated in the ears of the stunned priest, for now Justo Granudo began to dance around in a circle, while playing on a small wooden flute that he had pulled from within his shirt. The dog also was scampering about and leaping up into the air as if playing with its master. There was no indication of an injury. The priest was almost convinced that his eyes had deceived him or that it had been a performance put on by man and dog. Suddenly, the animal again, as unexpectedly as before, leaped at Justo. This time it bit into the neck. Man and animal rolled on the muddy ground. Father Rodrigo saw the flesh being torn. The initial shock lasted but a second. The priest commenced savagely beating the dog away from the victim. Whimpering, the animal cowered away. The priest having worked himself into a frenzy did not stop until he heard a note from the flute. Turning, he saw Justo standing and once again playing the instrument.

"Who are you?" the priest shouted, confused and overwhelmed by fear.

Justo did not answer but kept playing the flute.

The priest shouted the question again, his voice cracking.

Justo Granudo looked up with a pained expression. "You don't trust me," he said.

The priest immediately felt that he had given offence. Justo, a cruel look on his face, stepped menacingly forward. Father Rodrigo turned and ran all the while hearing the man and the dog running after him. Everything reeled. He felt his fingers grasping the mud. There was a taste of earth and blood in his mouth. His head stung.

When he came to, he was aware of a mild ache all over his body. He lay on the ground a while as if resting. Remembering what had happened, he quickly got up, looked around, and seeing nothing out of the ordinary, he hurried home, and getting there, he locked himself in. The next day he wrote a letter to the bishop, and shortly thereafter he was relieved of his duties at Rio Alto.

The Homeless Man

When I arrived at work one morning, Mildred approached me. "I took a different route to work this morning," she said to me.

"It's always good to explore," I said in an attempt to keep the conversation light. Her face seemed to express something of more import than her route to work. Whatever came up next was bound to be more bizarre than everyday office banter, though, with her, that too leaned toward the unusual.

"Well, I thought I'd explore your route across town."

"Which one? I do vary my steps from time to time."

"You know, across on 47th Street."

"Ah," I said, "through the jewelry district."

"That wasn't the interesting part," she said. "I'm talking about closer to here. You know, where the homeless guy hangs out."

I had mentioned the homeless person to her once, expressing my curiosity about how he kept his wardrobe so presentable. He hangs out on 47th Street between Madison and Park. I see him there every morning as I walk from the subway on Sixth Avenue to my office on Lexington. He is there all year round. I wonder how he can stand the winter cold. He's relatively well-kept and seems to have a placid personality. His face is round and pudgy, and always he bears a calm expression. He has several duffle bags stacked one on top of the other and covered with cardboard boxes to protect them from the elements. Sometimes, he talks to himself. Very often people give him money or cigarettes without him asking. There is something about him that does not repel people as is often the case with other homeless persons. There is something childlike about him that disarms the passersby.

At lunchtime, I sometimes see him near 49th and Third where there are benches. He sits writing in a notebook, the type that has the black and white squiggles on the stiff cover. He writes diligently. It makes me think that he is educated. Perhaps he is keeping a diary of his life in the street, or maybe he's writing a novel.

His life must be hard, and yet it must have some advantages. He has no one to answer to, no boss to harangue or intimidate him, no fear of unemployment, no one depending on him for sustenance. He has no responsibilities but to keep himself alive, and he seems to have no anxiety about that, or about anything else. Perhaps he never did, and that's how he ended up in the street. Anxiety spurs us on to fulfill our duties, however we envision them. Maybe we are born with an anxiety gene, and if it is missing, or shuts off, then we lack a necessary component to function successfully in society.

Who is to say that our man on 47th Street is not successful enough? He hasn't starved. He is always clean and his clothes look presentable enough. Where does he bathe and shave? He obviously has a haircut regularly. All of this does not happen on 47th Street. He must have a whole other life about which I know nothing.

I decided to take the light approach in the discussion with Mildred. "I see," I said, "you're trying to expand your social circle."

"Actually, you're right. I can look in either direction. You know that there is no absolute up and down in the universe?"

"Well, I suppose it's all relative, isn't it?"

"Precisely, sometime I underestimate your genius."

"On that, I won't contradict you," I said.

"Anyway, I think he could be an interesting project."

"For a social worker you mean."

"For anybody," she responded.

"Ah, have you anybody in mind, Dreiser perhaps?" Dreiser was our department supervisor who had a Machiavellian approach to doing his job.

"This isn't a humorous situation," she countered.

"Yes, you're right about that, so who are you planning to enlist?"

"I have a friend who likes to take on social projects," she said.

I figured that listening to Mildred was a major social problem. On my way to work the next day, I saw the homeless man still at his post. I concluded that Mildred's project to ameliorate his condition had not yet made an impact; but of course, how can she have gotten anything done so quickly? At midmorning, she came over and sat by my desk. She had a grin on her face that imported a rise in self-satisfaction, a condition she was fond of displaying.

"Guess what?" she said.

I gazed at her thinking that the question was rhetorical and that the answer would come from the same source as the question, but she merely stared at me waiting for my verbal response to the insufficient clue.

"I spoke to my friend, Karen, and she is interested in taking on the project."

"The project?" I questioned, though I knew perfectly well that she was referring to the homeless man on 47th Street. It seemed a bit strange that the situation had progressed to the status of a project. How large a project was it going to be? Was a whole team to be assembled to deal with the various aspects of it? Was it the inception of a social movement that would expand to include all of Manhattan and then spill over into the other boroughs? I surmised that it would be welcomed in the Bronx but not on Staten Island. I had never imagined that there were any homeless people in Queens and so few in Brooklyn that a move to deal with them would be unnecessary. Of course, all of this was speculative, and in all probability completely inaccurate. If I wanted an answer, research would have to be done, but I was not really interested in the numbers, but merely in Mildred's response to the situation. Her bringing another person into the scheme added another dimension. I knew nothing about this person other than Mildred's assertion of her interest in social projects. I imagined that this person was an activist left over from the Sixties, one who had not shed the social consciousness that had flourished in those days.

"Yes, the project," she said. "Of course, it's a small one. It's only one homeless person we're talking about when there are hundreds in the city, perhaps several thousands. I don't have any statistics on this. I better look it up," she said. She reached over to my desk to appropriate a page from a note pad that conveniently rested there for the use for any visitor who wished to take notes on our conversation. I presumed that my opinion was worthy of being written down and that many guests were more than happy to have the opportunity to do so. I, being so accommodating, kept my note pad handy for their use.

"I presume your friend has a plan in mind, and she has, of course, imparted it to you," I said, and immediately regretted the fatuous tone that inadvertently colored that statement.

"Well, you sound like you have an attitude," she said.

"I apologize," I said. "It's just that the situation is rather overwhelming in scope."

"Well you know, 'A journey of a thousand miles begins with one step.'"

"Ah, yes, I sometimes forget that you're a Maoist."

"A what?"

"Never mind," I said. "So what's your friend's plan?"

"Well, the first thing is to find the homeless guy a place to live."

"Don't you first have to get him to agree to get off the streets?"

"Well, that goes without saying."

"And you think that's the simple part of the process."

"Simple? Nothing in the world is simple."

"I think you're making progress. I suppose that your friend Karen is connected to some organization that handles homeless people."

"No, not at all."

"Ah," I said and dropped the subject.

Several weeks later the homeless man was still at his usual spot on 47th Street. I wondered whether Mildred's friend had yet to find some way to execute her plan or whether, on thinking it over, she had concluded that New York was not New Delhi and that her resemblance to Mother Theresa was too farfetched.

"Perhaps I'm being a bit harsh on someone who is attempting to be a Good Samaritan," I said.

"A what?" Mildred asked, her tone conveying some annoyance.

"Ah, nothing," I said. "Your friend's magnanimity is to be admired."

"It certainly is," she retorted, still in a harsh tone.

"My, my, you're in a testy mood today."

"You're right. I'm having one of those days."

I figured she was referring to a female biological process, so I didn't further inquire about her discomfort.

On my way to work on Monday, I noticed that the homeless guy was not at his post. I figured that he was probably taking a day off. We all need a vacation once in a while, or perhaps he had certain number of sick days allotted to him by his employer, and he was taking advantage of that perk. He wasn't there the next day either so I mentioned it to Mildred.

"I know," she said. "He seems to have disappeared. Karen is rather distraught. She had determined to keep trying to assist him. Success is a big deal to her, no matter what the project."

"Well, then I'm sorry for both of them," I said. "But I'm sure she'll recover. There are plenty of homeless people around. She can attach herself to someone else."

"You're your usual witty self today," she said.

"I can't help it," I said. "It comes naturally."

She made a face and walked away.

About a year later, at The 8th Street Book Store, as I perused the books on the best sellers table, I noticed the title *Homeless on 47th Street.* I picked up the book and turned it over to read the synopses on the backside of the jacket, and there it was, a photograph of the author, the homeless man.

Going Home

WHEN I STARTED out to visit my place of birth, I did not expect anything extraordinary to happen. In fact, when I spoke to anyone about how wonderful my childhood memories were and how I remembered the grandiose landscape and the little towns tucked away in the central mountains, everyone warned me that I would be disappointed, not because the island didn't have its wondrous and beautiful settings, but because memory tends to conspire with imagination to create quite fantastical things out of the past. "Besides," everyone said, "things have changed. Twenty years is a long time, and the world doesn't stand still. Most of what you remember probably doesn't exist anymore."

I somewhat agreed. I tried to prepare myself for the tricks of memory. I examined my recollections for the slightest tinges of romanticism, and I discounted the suspects. I stuck to what I thought was harsh reality. Still, twenty years of memory is a long distance for reality to travel.

Yes, twenty years ago my family moved to New York. My father came here to escape his creditors, or if not, at least a poverty that would have destroyed him, and perhaps, in one way or another, the whole family, though now when anyone mentions it, he assumes a look that says, "Maybe that was the reason and maybe not." Life in New York was not an immediate improvement. In fact, in many ways it was worse. We arrived in the Autumn. We had never before experienced cold weather. My mother suffered the most.

She did not like living in an apartment, cloistered, and having to keep the door always locked. The fact that she did not speak English was a great discomfort to her—a woman who was used to being heard. She had enjoyed haggling with shopkeepers at the markets, but now she could not even speak to them.

My father's hometown, Rio Alto, is nestled in a valley in the middle of the mountain range that runs from one end of the island to the other. The town was so small that it had only two streets, and some paths and alleyways on a steep hill—the poorer section, which looked as if it was about to slide down on the rest of the town. We had relatives in town, but most lived up the mountain. Back then, as soon as we got off the public car, I was eager to start on the path up the side of the slope to my grandfather's house. In my memory, that house was more like a castle from where my grandfather, a powerful sorcerer, ruled a vast and magical domain. The house, an impressive wooden structure, was like the great hall of ancient lord, with the kitchen at one end and sleeping quarters on the other. It had no modern conveniences—no electricity, no running water. Cooking was done over an open fire on a sand table.

In the morning the smoke rose, curled about the kitchen rafters and formed into the ephemeral shapes of beasts and demons. Outside someone fed the geese, the chickens and watered the flowers while I romped until breakfast was ready. One time, after breakfast, my grandfather showed me how to get resin glue by slashing the bark of a tree, and we used the glue to construct a toy cart. Sometimes we walked along the mountain path from where we could see the town in the distance below, the tin roofs of the houses shining in the sun, like jewels encrusted in the green landscape. In the woods, he lifted me off the ground to look into a birds nest with two little speckled eggs in it. Then home we walked, as he told me stories of haunted places in the forest.

These memories emerged when after a twenty years absence, I was about to visit my homeland. I looked forward to the romanticism of childhood that awaited me at the other end of that plane trip.

"Please, calm yourself. You're bound to be disappointed," my wife said to me. "You've worked yourself up to expect too much."

"I'm perfectly aware of that danger," I assured her. "I've prepared myself."

Cousin Tito greeted us at the airport. Once we had the baggage, he whisked us to his car, and I was off on my journey into the past. Thinking that I would be disappointed, my wife maintained a worried look.

"Is the hospital still where it used to be?" I asked as we rode.

"What hospital?"

"Where my father used to work?"

"No, there's a housing development there now. They moved the hospital to a larger building somewhere else."

"Oh," I said. My wife flinched.

"I think I'll drive up to Rio Alto tomorrow," I continued cautiously.

"You'll be able to drive up the mountain. They built a road where the path used to be."

"That's nice," I said.

"And now that there's electricity and everything, lots of people have vacation homes up there."

I was quiet and just looked out the window. I did not recognize anything. As we entered Baronin, I was absolutely resigned. The town seemed to have been completely rebuilt, and it was now so much more bustling than I had dreamt possible.

The next day I felt better, having determined that I would not let that silly obsession of finding my childhood prevent me from enjoying myself. We rented a car and after carefully studying a road map we set out for Rio Alto. On the road things looked much better than they had the day before. Getting into the rural parts of the island revealed the greenness that I remembered. The road curved and twisted along the top of the ravines at the bottom of which coursed sparkling streams. Yes, it was still here. My wife touched my arm.

"What is it?" I asked.

"You're stepping on the gas a little too hard," she said.

I was excited. All the resolve I had in the morning melted away, and I was again trying to reach into the past. I was not as disappointed with Rio Alto as I had been with Baronin. There was nothing there that I recognized either, but at least the town had not grown into a metropolis. We parked the car and walked around.

"There are more sidewalks, and the church is a lot smaller than I thought," I said to my wife.

"We shouldn't have come here," she said, "Now you'll be depressed the rest of the day. Let's not drive up the mountain."

I agreed, and we went to visit some people who had been my mother's friends. They asked us to stay the night. After dinner, I decided to take a walk through the town again. My wife was too tired to accompany me, so I left her with our hosts, and I set out alone. Before long I was heading toward the edge of town and up the mountain road. "I'll just go a short way," I said to myself. Night was coming on, and I heard the crickets in the grass by the side of the road. Fireflies flew around me in erratic patterns. Was this the way it was long ago? I lost myself in reverie trying to correlate what I was experiencing with what I remembered. I do not know how long I walked before I noticed the lights of the town below me. I was about to turn back when I saw, on the other side of the road and across a small field, the ruins of a house. I debated whether I had enough time to look it over. I didn't want to walk back to town in pitch darkness.

A figure seemed to emerge from the ruin and beckoned to me. The man was short and rather stocky, streaks of grey in his abundant hair, dark eyes under bushy eyebrows. "Ignore him," flashed through my mind, but a dog trotted up and began to bark as if it recognized me. That caught my interest.

"I was about to give up waiting," he said.

He addressed me in a familiar tone. That, and his words, surprised me, since I did not know who he was. Besides, no one knew I would be walking up this way.

"Waiting for what?"

The man did not answer. The dog licked my hand.

"If you're waiting for someone, I'm the wrong person," I said.

"You're Mencio's boy," the man said.

"No," I said stunned. Mencio was my grandfather's name.

The man ignored the answer and kept talking. "I do what I have to, and so I waited for you."

I was about to protest again but the continued, "Here's the house. Come!"

He led the way as we entered what had once been a house. He took out a bamboo flute from inside his shirt and began to play. The dog moved around him as if it were dancing.

"That's a well-trained dog you have," I said.

"You trained him," the man said.

"I don't know what you mean," I answered. "I never saw you or that dog before."

I must have stumbled on the neighborhood lunatic or else on a practical joker. Either way I was uneasy. What would he get into his head next? I was relieved when he said, "I must leave you now. I'll take care of the dog until you return."

"I'm not returning," I said sardonically to myself.

"Until you return to stay," he continued, "this belongs to you."

He bent down and from behind a pile of wood he produced a toy cart like the one my grandfather had once made for me. My wife must have hired this man, I thought indignantly turning around and walking away from him. But she did not know I would be walking up there. When would she have had time to do it? I had been with her all day. I turned around to ask him. He was gone, nowhere to be seen.

Back in town I recounted the story. My wife disclaimed all responsibility. My host and hostess said that they did not know anyone that fit the description I gave them. I was mystified. The next day we went around town inquiring about the man and the dog. No one knew anything. Finally, we gave up, and we spent the rest of our vacation in places I had never visited before.

The Mother Tongue

Rebecca Brown worked as an interviewer at one of the Employment Service offices in the Bronx. She was a blond and blue eyed young woman, born and raised in Virginia. In college she had majored in Spanish and was fluent in the language. After graduation, she moved to New York. She was single, and everyone in the office tried to introduce her to prospective partners. She never had a second date, giving rise to the consensus that she suffered from frigidity.

"That's not an insurmountable problem," Lydia once said when, in Rebecca's absence, some of the staff discussed the matter.

"I agree," Antonio said. "The right man would get her going."

"And you're volunteering?"

"She's not my type," he emphatically announced to make clear that he was beyond dealing with damaged goods.

"Well, maybe you're not her type either," Lydia continued. "She's not someone you can push around to your heart's content."

"I think she has a soft spot for Mario," Antonio said.

"I'm taken," Mario said.

"Margarita is not available," Antonio chimed in. For some reason, he was obsessed with commenting on Mario's attraction to the receptionist.

"That's a matter of opinion," Lydia said.

"I'm referring to Isabel," Mario emphasized.

Mario did find Rebecca physically attractive, but something about her made him wary. His reserve had nothing to do with the rumor of her having a sexual problem, which in those days he viewed as a malady that had a simple remedy. Something else about Rebecca disturbed him. The exact nature of the problem, difficult to pinpoint, had something to do with her attachment to the Spanish language. Her speaking the language fluently, at first perceived as a positive attribute, soon revealed an enigmatic side of her, an obsession. She often insisted on using Spanish when everyone else was speaking English. Mario suspected that her attraction to him stemmed from that fixation, and a more intimate relationship with her would hinge on constantly speaking in his native tongue and not in hers.

"What does that matter?" Antonio said when Mario confided his observation of this quirk in her character. "So you speak to her in Spanish while you hump. What's the big deal?"

"I want women to love me, not the language I speak."

"Joe Schmo," Antonio retorted. "I'm not saying you should marry her. She just needs to get laid."

"I'll pass on this one. Besides I have Isabel to think about."

"I'm telling you," his colleague continued. "You'll be sorry."

In appearance, Rebecca was unquestionably a beautiful woman. Back when they were first hired, during orientation week, another rookie made his attraction to her very obvious. He constantly made comments about her good looks, compliments she found annoying coming from a clown. Obviously, he lacked self-control, unable to repress the words that everyone else held like dogs on a tight leash. Mario, too, that first week noted Rebecca's good looks, and he might have chased after her, had he not already fixated on Isabel. Rebecca's oddity, unlike her physical beauty, which was visible across the room, was much less obvious. On closer examination, her personal quirks become evident except to those with their own loose screw. Initially, Mario sensed something strange about her, but he could not pinpoint exactly what.

Antonio kept pointing out to Mario her obvious interest in him. "You're blind," Antonio repeated to his friend, but Mario found Antonio's observation unverifiable. "I'm telling you, she has the hots for you," became Antonio's refrain. "And nothing makes it more obvious than her flop in the restaurant."

He was referring to the time when the staff had arranged to go out to lunch, and Isabel, Mario's interest at the time, at the last moment, decided to join them, intending afterwards to continue to Kingsbridge to visit her mother. Seeing Isabel in the restaurant startled Rebecca, and as if she were a competitive ice skater attempting to learn a new routine, the distraction caused her to slip and hit the floor. No one else had a problem with the texture of the floor, and anything amiss with Rebecca's shoes was unverifiable. Even she did not bother to blame her shoes. Totally disoriented, she remained the focus of attention, a role Isabel usually played without effort or intention.

A year later, Mario left the Employment Service, and he didn't see Rebecca again for some time.

Isabel departed on a trip to California to visit her sister. So one evening without a companion, he found himself at the 92nd Street Y attending a reading by a Latin American poet.

Once seated, he looked to his right and spied Rebecca down the aisle from him. He looked straight at her and their eyes met. He waved to her. She turned her head and pretended not to have seen him.

He had failed to wave in Spanish.

Lunch in San Juan

Tomas Además sat in the front seat of the Chevrolet as it moved slowly through the outskirts of San Juan towards the center of the city. In the morning he had taken a shower, washed his hair before applying the brilliantine that allowed him to shape it to enhance his masculine look. In his youth he had worked in the fields, had worn a straw hat until he discovered that showing off his hair combed in a particular way made women take a second look. He had been only a teenager then, but the habit of plastering his hair with the shiny substance persisted. After he married, he felt he needed the look to keep his wife happy and to remind her that other women looked at him also.

The morning that he was to ride into San Juan, his wife served him breakfast as usual. She had buttered the bread for him and had placed it on the left side of the plate that held the two eggs fried "*bombita en cima.*" The cup next to the plate contained half milk half coffee. He sat at the table to eat even though the smell of the food made him nauseous. He had not slept well, but that seemed to be having a result adverse to the usual.

"Eat your breakfast," she said.

"I'll throw up," he answered.

"Don't go today," she said.

The hesitancy in her voice proved to him that she really wanted him to go. He would make his mark on the world that day. His name would appear in the history books, but more importantly he would prove to her that he was a man beyond the ordinary.

"You don't have to prove anything," she said.

"You read my thoughts?"

"It's simple enough to read what you put on your face."

"Everything will be all right," he said.

"I know," she answered.

He heard the sound of motor vehicles pulling up in front of the house, and he gazed at the briefcase on the floor next to the book cabinet; on the top shelf rested the RCA radio through which surely she would hear the news. The briefcase held the army pistol he had acquired at a very good price. Getting weapons was simple enough. Rifles could be ordered through the Sears Roebuck catalogue, although that was not how he had obtained the pistol. He had bought it from someone who worked in the Santurce American army base. That was ironic. They would be struck with their own weapons, although a real American was not this time the target.

The two cars had stopped in front of his house, but no one emerged to knock on the door. They waited for him to come out on his own. He kissed his wife on the forehead, a gesture, as if in a soap opera with him the romantic hero and her the heroine for whom a man would do anything. Yes, he would do anything for her, and although what he was doing now was for everyone, he knew that she appreciated his role. All of her life she had been a supporter of independence. Her father had believed in it, and she had followed without question, sometimes even more emotional about it than the old man had ever been. Her mother said little but always did her duty supporting the husband's point of view. Migdalia had her own stance and she would not change it for any man. It was often the same as her father's, but she claimed that to be incidental. He just happened to be right.

Once in the car, Tomas was thankful for the short distance from Rio Piedras to San Juan. On route there was nothing really to talk about. All the planning had been done and everyone understood the danger of the enterprise. Only distraction was necessary to keep fear at bay. Raimundo, in the front seat with the driver, did most of the talking. Once in a while he turned his head back to glance at Tomas.

"This is our moment of glory," he said, winking at Tomas, "So put a smile on your face."

*

At the dock, Don Fernando bought the ferry tickets. As they walked up the gangplank, the boy, holding on to his father's hand, gazed down into the green water. At the edge of the dock, boys in shorts, their wet hair plastered to their foreheads, enticed by coins thrown by the ferry passengers, waited to dive again. Grinning, their teeth shining, they dove and emerged holding up the retrieved coins.

"Here, throw in a nickel," Don Fernando said to his son.

The boy pondered to which of divers he should throw the nickel, while they loudly urged him to throw it in. Giving up trying to decide which one should get it, he closed his eyes and threw it up in the air to let chance decide. Two of the boys dove once they determined where the coin might hit the water, the others stayed in place to await the next toss. Almost immediately, the two who had dived resurfaced, one holding the coin up to show his success.

A peanut vendor walked by the isle crying out, "*Mani, maní asado!*" Again, Don Fernando put his hand in his pocket to pull out a coin. He passed it to the vendor who handed over a small bag of roasted peanuts. "Here, you hold the bag," Don Fernando said to his son. "I'll crack them for you."

"All right," the boy said, handing a peanut up to his father.

Father and son stood by the side rail to watch the dock attendants lift the heavy-rope loops from the mooring. From the boat, another attendant pulled up the ropes winding them on the cleats.

"Now we're going," Don Fernando said.

As the ferry backed away from the dock, the boys in the water swam after it hoping more coins would be thrown in, but most passengers had moved away from the railings to find seats in the cabin. The boy and his father moved up to the front to watch the bow plow through the water creating froth as it went. The boat moved further from the shore, and after a short distance the color of the water darkened.

"Look over there," Don Fernando said pointing to birds that flew low over the waves. Suddenly one dove and emerged with a still flipping fish firmly in its beak. The boy was astounded as another bird dove and also came up with a fish.

"What do they do with the fish?"

"They eat it. It's their lunch."

"Guts and all?" The boy inquired, remembering his mother in the kitchen cleaning out the insides of a fish before frying.

"Of course," the father said.

On arriving at the other side of the bay, the boat slowly approached the dock. The attendant hoisted the docking rope and threw it out to a fellow worker on shore who placed the loop over the mooring post. After performing that at the bow, they moved to the stern at a quick pace to repeat the process there. The gangplank went down with a clank as the passengers lined up to disembark.

The boy firmly held on to his father's hand. His heart beat faster. The view of the world momentarily curtailed was soon restored as the passengers' descent to the dock dissolved the fear of being smothered.

"Here we are," Don Fernando said. "This is the big town."

The houses leading up to the docks had no space between them, each touching the other. Seeing the two story structures for the first time, the boy was amazed, and even more so when he gazed up at a three story ones, but as if height was not enough to marvel, some of the facades were covered halfway up with brightly colored tiles.

"Tall house," the boy said.

"You think so?" In New York there are buildings that touch the sky."

The boy heard his father's words, but he failed to let them evoke an image. The buildings in front of him now, in the narrow stone paved streets, were enough to occupy his imagination. They walked through a small park that featured a little animal caged in an enclosure built around the trunk of a tree. "That's a squirrel," Don Fernando said to the boy. "There are many of those in America, but that's the only one here."

The boy stared at the bushy-tailed creature that now and again scurried up the tree and on reaching the top of the enclosure and finding no place else to go, scurried down again. Father and son walked across and out of the small park, down a narrow street into the business part of the city.

They stopped at a corner restaurant.

"Here we can have some American food," Don Fernando said.

They sat at a table and Don Fernando spoke to the young waiter who smiled down at the boy who, except for cornflakes, had never eaten American food before.

"Oh, you'll like American cheese," he said to the boy who wondered what could possibly make cheese American. He knew white cheese, which was watery and eaten at Christmas with guava, and there was the hard round cheese eaten at all other times. As far as he knew only those two kinds of cheeses existed in his world that consisted of only three places: this island where he lived; Spain, from where Columbus had sailed to discover the island; and America, to where people now went never to be seen again.

The waiter returned with the order. "Cheese sandwich for you," he said to the boy, who stared at the strange forms on the plate. He had never seen that kind of bread before, white, flat, and evenly grained. Between the bread slices, diagonally cut into two triangles, protruded an ornate toothpick that looked like a *banderilla* stuck on a bull in the arena, something he had seen in photographs.

"Go ahead and taste it," his father said.

The combination of the white bread and dark yellow cheese had a novel taste, pleasant enough though not something he would look forward to having again the way he longed for those yellow rolls of bread the priest had given out in school one day. The boy had loved that bread, but there was no place in town to buy it, and he could not figure out how Father Alfonso had obtained it.

"Now that's an American sandwich," Don Fernando said, winking at his son.

*

In an attempt to prevent nausea from overcoming him, Tomas looked straight ahead through the front window as if he were driving the auto. Today he had been nauseous even before getting into the car, one of the reasons why he had been reluctant to eat, though he had failed to explain that to Migdalia: without breakfast he would have nothing to throw up. But with no food, just bodily bile would emerge and that would be equally unpleasant.

"There's nothing to worry about," Raimundo said, "We'll be in and out in no time at all. Think of it as your lucky day."

Tomas thought about what luck might mean. The first part was to hit the target. The Governor's Palace was a huge place. How would they know what room he was in? While planning, they had assumed that he would be in his office, but there was no way to assure that. On their arrival, he might be in the men's room. If there was more than one near his office, which one did he use? Would the location of a private one be apparent? Tomas imagined the governor in the bathroom emptying his bladder. In that pose he was a man just like anyone else. What right had anyone to kill him? Had God delegated the right to take a life without the permission of the state or the church? The state was in enemy hands, so then only the Pope could approve such an act, and there was no such approval. Don Pedro, the party leader who planned and ordered the attack, was a devout Catholic, but he had no document from the Pope authorizing the liquidation of anybody. If he had, he had failed show it or even mention it. To kill was a mortal sin, and yet to kill the enemy was a necessity. The nausea brought up the dilemma: too late to change his mind even if he had a change of heart. But the discomfort of traveling in a car, the nausea, caused by moving faster than was natural for a human, might really be the problem, having nothing to do with the mission that was, after all, meant in good will as a gift to the people. That too had a moral sustenance. God had made us a people, and we had the right to keep God's will from being thwarted.

On reaching the city, they drove along Avenida de Cristobal Colon. The day suddenly took on a brightness Tomas had not expected, as if he had never before been through these streets. The sunlight revealed to him details that he had ignored until that moment, when he lacked the leisure to take a closer look at what had been there all of his life. Yellow seemed to be the dominant color, giving the city a golden hue, as they moved into the old section that had been there for several centuries. An internal voice urged Tomas to close his eyes. Everything he saw was an urge against what he was about to do. If he closed his eyes, he would keep the reflection of the sun on the historic stones from altering his purpose.

"What if the gates are closed?" Raimundo asked Enrique, the driver, as if the thought had just entered his mind and the subject had not been discussed before. Indeed it had, and it had been decided that if that were the case, Pepe, who was riding in the lead car, was to rush the gate and force it open after shooting the guards.

"It'll be open," Enrique said.

That quieted Raimundo. The car turned into Calle Fortaleza, and the gate came into view.

*

"We'll take a walk down to the Governor's Palace," Don Fernando said to the boy as they emerged from the restaurant.

"El Morro?" the boy asked.

"No, that's an old fort. In the old days it kept away the pirates. Now it's just a sight for the tourists."

"Are we tourists?"

Don Fernando laughed. "We're citizens, so we'll visit the governor."

As father and son approached the corner of Fortaleza and San Jose, two autos were slowly progressing down the narrow street.

"We'll just follow those cars taking important people to meet with the governor."

"Will he see us?"

"Sure, he will. I voted for him, and you'll vote for him when your turn comes."

"All right," the boy said.

Walking down Fortaleza, Don Fernando observed that one of the automobiles stopped, and one of its riders stepped out to look at the right rear wheel. "It looks fine," the man said. "Check the other side," the driver instructed. The checker walked behind the vehicle to inspect the tire on the left side. He gazed at it intently to assure that he was making an accurate observation. "We haven't got all day," the driver shouted as Don Fernando and his son passed by. The driver looked up, and he turned his face away in annoyance as if he were in danger of losing a race to the palace and would lose his turn to see the governor.

"We'll get there first," Don Fernando said to the boy, who remained unaware of what his father meant.

*

The gate was indeed closed.

"*Carajo*!" Raimundo exclaimed as if he had expected an easy entrance.

"Calm down, Pepe will take care of it," Enrique assured him as the auto came to a halt.

A few seconds elapsed before they realized that the second car was not immediately behind them.

"*Coño*, he's not here," Raimundo said. He opened the car door and stepped out before Enrique could stop him. Raimundo kept his weapon lowered as he walked to the other side of the car, but once there he lifted it and fired at the lock.

"He's insane," Enrique said also stepping out, weapon in hand.

Two guards had immediately responded from the gate but one had fallen. Now there was gunfire coming from the second story of the palace. Just as the second car pulled up, Tomas, on the side away from the building, emerged from the auto. He turned to see Raimundo fall, the force of the bullets pushing his body backward causing him to fall face up gazing at the sky. Enrique too was hit and expletives emerged from his mouth as he kept firing. Tomas considered

throwing down his gun and putting up his hands, but fire was still coming from the second car and surely they must have noticed that he had not yet fired a single shot. They would tell Migdalia that he had done nothing, and her disdain would render his death meaningless. The second car, instead of backing up and taking flight, was still there, and Tomas took that as a sign of their courage. In reality, the driver had been hit, and his body lay over the steering wheel making it impossible at the moment to regain control of the automobile.

Tomas raised his weapon and was about to turn and fire when he noticed the man and the boy stunned into paralysis by the action in front of them. "Lie down, you fools!" he shouted at them, forgetting for an instant that the danger he was pointing out to them was a threat to him also. He moved from behind the auto towards the unexpected viewers, but suddenly remembering where he was, he turned to fire. He was startled by the strange effect of his action. On hearing the sound caused by the explosion that propelled the bullet, he was suddenly confronted with a view of the sky, across which a solitary bird seemed to be progressing toward an eternal destination.

The Nymph

THE TWO STREETS town was snugly nestled at the foot of the mountain. The main street ran through the middle of the conglomeration of houses, and the other wound along the river and merged with the longer one halfway through town. The sun beat down on the tin roofs of the huddled houses that seemed to be whispering to each other. As a child, I had an intense dislike for the town with its rundown structures and squalid alleys where, in the rain, half naked children played in the mud.

Visiting relatives who lived on the mountain was an irksome duty, so when my parents took me there, I was always eager to leave town and start up the trail to Grandfather's house, where I was sometimes left when my parents needed time for themselves. Each stay in that house was an adventure for me; it was so austere that my imagination was free to embellish it at will. From the inside, the bare beams and rafters made its strength clearly visible. In the morning, I would lie on my bed looking at the wisps of smoke from the kitchen curl about the rafters and form into nebulous shapes that would seep out through the thatched roof to disappear forever. I was fascinated by the free and uncontrollable nature of that smoke, more intractable and transparent than the clouds in the sky, which my imagination often forced into recognizable forms.

My grandfather was like the house, impressive and austere in appearance. In spite his age, he was slim and strong, and his bronzed countenance bore a look of unshakable determination, as if it were carved from some stone that would forever resist the assault of time and weather. He projected his authority with a glance, so that when anyone in the household committed any peccadillo, the perpetrator tried to disappear for a while, hoping that Grandfather would accumulate more pressing matters to attend to. The old man seldom lost his temper, but everyone feared the devastating look that implanted guilt and remorse. I sometimes had the impression that I detected the same quality in my father and hoped that it was a hereditary trait that would eventually be manifested in me, but I have long since concluded that the characteristic must be acquired through long experience in the world.

On a horse, Grandfather cut a dashing figure. Watching him ride out to inspect the tobacco fields, I saw the movement generated by the bones and sinews of the animal mysteriously transferred to the man. Like an electrical cell storing power, he retained within him the energy generated by the animal. He was a man easily idolized by those who knew him only casually. He was what scores of women wished their husbands were and their sons would become. In his younger days many of them had succumbed to his forceful character, a fact attested to by several illegitimate scions, all with different mothers. This behavior was thought scandalous by the rest of the family, but there was no one to stand up to him. Everyone settled for talking behind his back.

My grandmother, as I gathered from snatches of overheard furtive whispers, suffered everything with remarkable resignation. Even the last know incident, which provoked from everyone more than the usual consternation, was weathered by my grandmother with remarkable equanimity. The furor arose from the unfortunate fact that the young woman involved committed suicide. As rumor had it, Grandfather got his favorite horse from the mayor of the town on a bet. He had long admired the animal, but the mayor had refused to sell it, and to still Grandfather's persistent queries had proposed an infamous wager. To earn the horse Grandfather had but to work his charm on Maria Chavez, a young lady renowned for her beauty and notorious for her chastity, the stipulation being that if he failed he was to stop importuning the mayor to sell the horse.

The scandalous talk began when Maria took her own life a few days after Grandfather was seen proudly riding home on the mayor's horse. That worthy official, of course, went up and down the town heatedly denying his complicity thus giving credence to the gossip. Grandfather behaved as if the talk were about someone else, never condescending to show whether he was giving the matter any thought. He was so nonchalant about it that eventually people began to doubt that he was guilty, and soon they conveniently forgot about the incident. Through all this, Grandmother impassively went about the household tasks and every Sunday, under the gaze of pitying neighbors, walking, rosary in hand, down the mountain trail to the parish church.

Though everyone believed that now the old man was ready to settle for simple domesticity, I occasionally heard my mother comment on those "shameless women" who came to the doors and windows of their houses to gaze at Grandfather ride by. In my childhood, all this talk was incomprehensible. To me, he was part of the land, like the hills and the trees, only more so. He had the power to move others, yet he was himself immovable. The trees were felled, and the land plowed. Rows of tobacco disfigured the sides of the hills. The town spread like a cancerous growth on the land, but the old man remained unchanged and unperturbed.

*

Occasionally, my parents took me along to visit friends or relatives who lived further up the mountain. Coming back along the ridge after dark, I marveled at the patterns of light that glowed against the velvet night from distant places that had already acquired electricity. When we got home, there would be a pot of chocolate on the fire and a buxom young woman standing in the kitchen ready to serve it. She was my aunt, but being young and good-natured, she did not demand from me the rigid conventions of respect that commonly go with that relationship. She told me jokes and played games with me, or she just told me stories while I gazed at the fire.

At dawn, looking into the distance, I saw the mist undulating along the contour of the land and covering the vegetation that clung to the earth like green fur on the limbs of a great beast. The mist disappeared each morning only to come back the next day; so that after a while, I gave up wondering where it came from and took it for a mystery like the Holy Trinity or the transmutation of bread and wine. When the mist cleared, the surface details of the country could be discerned more precisely, but for me it remained mysterious under its green wrap, my eyes traveling over the surface but never penetrating into the heart of the hills.

Because I was yet too young, those hills refrained from revealing to me some marvels that lurked on them, but at the time I only felt excluded as a stranger. Sometimes the women went into the forest to gather wood, and I stayed by the house waiting for the bent figures to return under enormous piles of dead branches. And when they talked of where they had been, I was filled with longing to see the places where the wood was gathered, but I was too young to carry anything and would only be in the way, besides I was a visitor, as if from another country, and everyone was convinced that given the slightest opportunity, I would get lost in the woods.

Yet the lure of the forest and of the unknown surroundings appealed to all the senses and was not to be ignored. Every day I wandered a little further from the house. Dew everywhere, my shoes became soaked as I tramped through the forest, the ground spongy from dead vegetation. Water sprinkled my face as I brushed through the shrubs. On some trees the bark had peeled to display random design made brilliant by the moisture. I sought them out right after rain or early in the morning before the dew evaporated. I would return from these excursions soaking wet, and everyone in the house would look at me and wonder at the strange obsession of walking through the wet underbrush.

There was a spot I avoided, an old fallen tree whose twisted trunk made it appear to be in violent contortion. Its unusual form and the golden brown color of the rotting wood, here and there covered with bright green moss, first attracted me. I walked around the tree examining it, running the tip of my fingers over its surface. The wood was brittle from age, and chunks of it chipped off at a touch. Suddenly, I was seized by a desire to see what was under it, though I had no reason to suppose there was anything unusual. I put all my efforts into rolling it over, and when I succeeded, I immediately recoiled in disgust. Hundreds of small worms writhed on the underside of the log and on the ground that it had covered. Their exposure to the light seemed to make them writhe more violently. Quickly I rolled the log back and hurried away from the spot.

Not too far into the forest there was a stream that cascaded down a natural inclination. Tiny fish, no bigger than half an index finger, their bodies composed of a clear gelatinous substance that revealed a bright red internal streak, swam about in the pool at the bottom of the fall. The little creatures looked like they were made of supple glass. I watched them swim around the stones covered with bright green algae. Going there often compensated for the unpleasant memory of discovering the secret of the log.

Sitting in the shade of the bamboo rushes on one side of the pool, I began to suspect that I was not the only one that frequented the place. On arrival, I had noticed that the sand in the pool had been disturbed and was in the process of once again settling to the bottom. The pool was not on Grandfather's property, and I doubted that anyone else from the house would stray that far for no apparent reason. Neither was there a trail leading to the place. The nearest house was that of *licenciado* Lopez, the wealthy neighbor, but he and his daughter did not spend much time there, so I had never met them, though I had heard much about the *licenciado*.

I was unwilling to give up the spot, and since after a while I noticed that little alteration resulted from sharing it with someone else, I decided to ignore the existence of the intruder. Occasionally, I noticed the grass bent where someone had stepped or lain on it, but it would always spring back. I had nearly forgotten about my fellow visitor, when one day on my way to the pool, I found a bird's nest on a low branch of a sapling. There were two eggs in the nest, and I was contemplating their spotted gray shells when I heard a voice behind me.

"Don't touch them or the mother birds won't come back to hatch them."

I turned around to behold a young woman smiling at me. She had been bathing in the pool, her hair wet and hanging down in thick strands over her plain brown dress. Her complexion was fresh and radiant, making me wonder whether she was human or some supernatural being, like the ones in the stories told to me at bedtime. She did not say another word but went on her way disappearing as if magically into the woods.

She continued her visits to the pool, and several times we ran into each other in the forest. On those occasions she invariably flashed a charming smile, but we seldom exchanged words. Only once, when she came upon me while I was examining some moss that grew at the base of a tree, did she speak at length. She knelt down beside me and began to tell me the names of the plants around us. Her voice had a musical quality, and I became engrossed in the sound of it and did not catch the meaning of her words. I only thought of how strange and beautiful she was. Back in the house, the return of our neighbor and his daughter from a trip abroad was discussed in vague terms, but I sensed an unusual sense of hostility. Intuitively, I knew to keep quiet about seeing her on my excursions.

One day on arriving at the waterfall, I stood within the bamboo grove. I was sure that she could not see me through the foliage, but she looked in my direction with her usual smile. My carefully wrought conscience capitulated without a struggle, and did not have the slightest compunction about staying to watch her take off her clothes. I thought of the tiny fish fleeing in all directions then stopping and from a safe distance tolerate the intrusion. The sun rays penetrated the foliage to illuminate her bare body. Her dark hair hung over her shoulder and some, reflecting the sunlight, resembled golden strands. She walked into the water shadowed by the bamboo thicket, the agitated sand at her feet rising in turmoil and settling down again. The backdrop of silence was torn by the cascading water and now and again was pierced by the hollow shriek of an indifferent bird. Her body deflected spray across patches of light that penetrated the foliage causing the colors of the rainbow to appear.

Hearing a rustling of leaves behind me, I turned and saw Grandfather's startled expression gradually turn into one of disappointment, then into rage. His angry face revealed a man deprived of pleasure he felt he earned through the anguish of anticipation. What right had a child to be concealed in the bamboo grove to deprive an old man of remnants of a miserable existence? He saw a conspiracy of fate, of time, of death creeping up to mock him. He dragged me away. How grotesque he seemed then—this old man venting his rage on life! In a moment of terror my eyes lost the power to see colors, and the old man became a frail shadow amid the towering monstrosities of the forest. He released me and, hoping to catch another glimpse of the young woman, he slinked back to the bamboo grove.

When I calmed down, I looked up at the sky to see the clouds transform into imaginary figures.

Gabi and Charlie

THE WAY GABI and Charlie was friends was strange. Nobody could understand it, 'cause they was always snapping on each other—like if they was mad at each other, but they wasn't. They was always together. Besides of which Charlie was crazy, everybody said so. Personally, I think Gabi was the crazy one. He had to be. Else why did he hangout with Charlie?

I never had nothing against Gabi. I liked him. "How come you always with Charlie?" I asked him. "Not that it's my business to tell you who you should hang out with, but for your own good, how come you always stick up for him?"

"I don' know," he said, "I don' know. He's all right."

Now, I gotta tell you that Gabi was no dummy. I got lots'a respect for a guy that's smart, and Gabi was smart—brainy, you know what I mean? He's the sort that would go a long way, if he had the chance. I don' say chance lightly, 'cause that's one thing I believe in: chance, luck, you know what I mean? What's gonna become of Gabi? I don' know, 'cause it all depends on if he gets a break or not. Eight or ten years from now when 1970 rolls around, and he's a man, he might be on top of the world, or he might be shooting dope or doing time. Never can tell. Some people never get no breaks. Don' get me wrong now; I don' mean like everything is luck. That's not what I mean at all. If a guy's got smarts, then he's gotta use 'em. He's gotta try, else he's not gonna get no place. But sometimes, lots'a times, you can try like the devil and still get no place. You can take it from me; that's the truth.

If a guy goes out'a his way to look for trouble, that's a different story. I don' know about Charlie. I don' wanna say that he was stupid, but he had a way of messing up. Like the day of the accident, it was all his fault. Gabi and me, we met him walking down the street holding a couple of cans of gasoline. Now if that ain't stupid, what is? If the cops had caught him they would'a beat the shit out'a him. They wouldn-t-ve had to; the shit would'a been coming out'a him before they even touched him. That fool would'a been shitting in his pants. Anyway, what happened was terrible, but let me start at the begining. You see, Charlie fell in with a bad bunch. That's not to excuse'm; he acted stupid, no doubt about that. I ain't trying to be like a mother, you know. Everybody's mother is the same. When a guy gets in trouble every mother blames his friends.

It all started with this storefront club called El Pueblo. Gabi, Charlie and me, we was heading down Lexington Avenue when we saw Gloria coming out'a this storefront where some guys was working to fix up the place. It looked like they was building a stage or something. Gloria pretended not to see us.

"Hey Gloria," Charlie called out, "what are they doing in there?"

She turned and snapped, "If you wanna know, go in and find out for yourself?" She looked at Gabi as if he had asked the question. I don' know what was going down between them, but she was sure as hell pissed at him.

“Don’ start up with me. He’s the one who wants to know,” Gabi said. He looked at her like he wanted to say something else, but he didn’t.

“What’s the matter? You all chicken to go in and ask?” said Gloria. She knew that she was getting Gabi’s goat.

“I ain’t chicken to ask, but I ain’t interested either,” Gabi said. “Around here they got storefronts for every goddamn thing. I ain’t interested in any of that stuff.”

“I am,” Charlie said. “Come on you guys. You gotta back me up.”

Gabi followed Charlie into the place, but he was still looking at Gloria as she walked away. I watched her also. That chick had a mean movement. I could’a watched her all day.

At first we only noticed two guys in the storefront. One was the carpenter. An electric saw was buzzing away. The second guy was sitting behind a desk. He was talking on the phone, maybe having an argument with someone, but it was hard to tell ‘cause’a the noise coming from the saw. We went up to the desk to wait for the man to get off the phone, but then we heard another voice.

“What can I do for you brothers?”

We was all startled, but the look on Charlie’s face was something else. Charlie was tall and puffy. He had eyes that glazed over when he was nervous. So there he stood looking like a giant Little Orphan Annie, Gabi and me standing behind him with our mouths open. The man who had spoken had a shaven head and sunken eyes. Strange! A bad looking dude! We had seen shaven heads before, and when we looked closely, he didn’t seem no different from everybody else. Still, you would'a thought he didn't have warm blood in his body. We hadn't seen him when we entered. Either he'd been sitting quietly in the dark corner or he had come in from another room.

"Welcome brothers, can I help you?"

We didn't say nothing.

"Just what we need," he said, "brothers who speak with the tongues of angels and of men."

"What are you? A preacher?" Charlie asked. "You building a church here, or something? You're wasting your time; too many churches around here already."

"Don' pay attention to him mister," Gabi said. "He's missing a couple of screws. We just wanna know about what this is gonna be."

I didn't say nothing. I didn't like the man. I got the feeling like he looked at people the same way he looked at cockroaches. I don' like to be looked at that way.

"The church of the proletariat. That's what we're gonna set up here."

"Well the Church of the Pentecost is just down the block, and they already have everybody signed up," Charlie said.

"As soon as we start giving out the champagne and caviar they'll all come over here," said the man who had been talking on the phone. He was smiling when he said that, so I figured it was some kind'a joke. But I didn't know what kind exactly. As far as I know they only serve champagne at weddings, but I never had any. Of course, in church you suppose'ta get bread and wine for communion. Champagne is like wine, but I never heard that caviar was a kind of bread. Someone told me it was goldfish eggs. I never even knew that fish laid eggs. When I heard that, I went to a pet shop every day for a week to look in the fish tank, but I never saw no eggs. Then I asked Eduardo Maldonado, who lives on my block, two buildings away. He has a tank full of fish, so I figured he would know. "Of course," he said. He looked at me as if I was really stupid, so I didn't ask him no more questions.

I didn't say any of that out loud. I was just thinking it to myself. It didn't seem to me like they was gonna make a church there anyway. Skullhead was just jiving us. The other man didn't look like no preacher. He looked like a regular guy. Like you knew right away that you could trust him. In his face he looked old, like if he was forty, but the way he moved and the way he talked was young, like twenty or so. I looked at him hard.

"Hey, I seen you before and you ain't no preacher," I said. "You're an actor, right?"

"Sometimes," he answered.

He stooped a little, made a face and with both hands twirled an imaginary moustache. "Ha, ha, ha, ha," he cackled. "The terror of 110th Street." He made like a phony villain. My eyes followed his movements. I caught sight of Skullhead in the corner. My heart skipped a beat. I couldn't believe how ugly he looked. The actor must've noticed my fright.

"Stop trying to scare people John," he said to Skullhead. "This is supposed to be a comic type villain, nothing to get ugly about."

Skullhead or John, whatever you wanna call him, personally he'll always be Skullhead to me, changed his expression right away. That seemed strange, ‘cause he’d been looking so mean. The minute the actor looked at him he changed, so I knew that as long as the actor was around John would be in check, but otherwise I wouldn’t wanna hangout with him. I was reminded of this movie I saw where a magician had power over an evil genie, and the genie was always trying to overcome him. The magician kept the genie around even though he was dangerous, and that’s one thing I’d never understand, ‘cause if it was me, I would’a cast a spell on that genie and imprisoned him in the middle of the earth. At first I thought of the usual method—putting him in a bottle and throwing it in the sea—but the bottle always washes up somewhere; some dumb bum opens it and the evil genie is out again. Though now that I think of it, I wouldn’t mind stuffing John in a bottle and throwin’m in the East River with the rest of the shit.

“That’s right,” Charlie said, “you did plays in the street last summer. Now I remember.”

“Right,” said the actor.

“They was all right,” Charlie said. “But I could’a done better. I was cut to be a great actor. So if you’re gonna do a play here, I wanna be in it.”

“Welcome to the troop,” the man said.

“Troop? I don’ wanna be no Boy Scout. I wanna be an actor!”

“Oh, listen to him,” Gabi said. “He’s so dumb I can’t believe it. Let’s get it all straight. Is this gonna be a church or a theater?”

“Neither and both,” said the man. “What we’re going to do is organize the neighborhood.”

"I just knew this was gonna be another one of those jive places," Gabi said. "Let's go."

"We need your help. Whose side are you on? What did a landlord ever do for you?"

"It sounds like jive to me," Gabi said. "Let's go."

"There'll be a block party on Saturday. Drop by!" said the actor.

That was the first time we met John, a.k.a. Skullhead, and Reinaldo, the actor, but that wasn't the last time. Personally, I think they was both crazy, but in different ways, know what I mean? This is just another hustle I thought when I heard this Reinaldo talk about fixing up the whole neighborhood. Cause, you know, every time you drop into one these storefronts there's someone there to tell you about a great idea, but when you're out in the street again you're just as likely to step in a pile'a of shit or have your guts slashed out by a mugger. I figured all those people with great ideas have one main one: to get somethin' for themselves and scram. I figured Reinaldo Guacamo wasn't no different, but I liked him. In lots of ways he knew where it was at.

2

On Saturday, Charlie, Gabi and me, we went to the block party to check out the action. When we got there, Flash and the Dynamics was settin' up their equipment. They play Latin rock, when they're not in jail. Flash is cool; he never gets into no trouble, but he can never keep his band together for very long 'cause, as I said, they keep gettin' busted, so it's always different guys with Flash, but in spite'a that they always sound good—most of the time.

"Wow, look at that!" Charlie shouted right in my ear.

"Will you cut that out," I pushed him away.

"Look, look!" he pointed and started walkin' very fast.

"What?" Gabi was gettin' annoyed too.

"Look over there! They have a pig," Charlie shouted.

An old man was turnin' a hog on a spit over coals. The spit had a crank at one end, and the old man, squattin', turned it. He was all red in the face and sweat rollin' down his forehead. It looked like the hog wasn't the only one gettin' done. A crowd of children stood around soakin' up the odor of the roastin' meat.

"So you never saw a pig before?"

"Not like that! Will you look! A stick through his ass, comes right out'a his mouth," Charlie was flabbergasted. He looked like his eyes was gonna pop right out'a his head.

"Hey, can I turn it?" he asked.

The old guy looked at him, then looked at the pig. He was thinkin' it over. Slowly he got up. I thought I heard his knees creak as he stood, figured he'd been squattin' there a long time. Charlie took his place, started turnin' the crank a little too fast."

"*Poco a poco, chico, poco a poco*," the old man said.

Charlie slowed down. The old guy grabbed a ladle that was stickin' out of a pot full of thick sauce. His fingers were long and knotty at the joints. His hand shook as he raised the ladle to pour the liquid over the pig. I thought he might spill some, but he didn't. He looked at me as if he'd seen what I was thinkin'. Embarrassed, I smiled. He poured the liquid like an artist, and it spread down the side of the pig like the sweat on the old man's face, but the skin of the pig was smooth. Some of the stuff dripped on the coals and sizzled.

"*Así era como lo hacíamos en Bayamón, así mismo*" the old man said to the children. They stared at him blankly.

"That means that's the way they did it in Bayamon, where he came from in P.R.," I said.

"*Yo lo se*," said a little girl.

"Yeah, big shot. We speak Spanish too, big shot," said a boy. His face was pale, eyes sunken, brown uncombed hair. He was the shortest kid in the group. I was gonna push his face in, but I figured it wouldn't do no good, so I didn't. I just stood there enjoyin' the smell of roast pig. Other smells began to blend in: *arroz con pollo* and *pasteles*. Wow! There was a lot of food bein' put out on tables. It was gonna be a feast, and I was gettin' very hungry just standin' there. The lot was fillin' up with people—men drinkin' beer, women settin' up tables, a large group in front of the bandstand. The musicians were bein' urged to hurry. I watched the people linin' up for food, and I waited to see if they had to pay, 'cause I didn't have a single penny. Soon as I was sure everythin' was free I stepped right up to get my share. Charlie was still turnin' the pig, and I had lost track of Gabi. I figured he'd gone to watch Flash and the Dynamics. I was stuffin' myself when I heard the music come over the loud speakers. The first blast made my hair stand on end. That was some powerful music. That music was gonna raise the lot through the darkness right up to the face of the moon. I could feel the ground risin'. People began to dance. What else can you do when the ground moves? The dancers helpin' the music, everyone wanted to get up there, close to the moon, away from the street, from the garbage, from the piss smellin' hallways. The people who were not dancin' began to clap their hands and stomp their feet. Yeah! It was risin'. I could feel it.

Reinaldo was dancin' too. I hadn't noticed him until then. His partner was wearin' a long dress of light material printed with red and orange flowers. Every time they danced across one of the lights in front of the bandstand the colors on the dress did a number. It was like the dress had caught fire. She moved like a flame. I never saw anyone move the way she moved.

"Hey, Gabi," I called out. He was standin' at the edge of the dancin' area watching Gloria dance with somebody else. He looked pissed.

"Did you eat? There's plenty of food over there, for nothin'," I said. People always feel better after they eat—no matter what's botherin' them.

"I ain't hungry," he said.

"Look at the broad Reinaldo is dancin' with. Ain't she wow?"

"Yeah," he said.

"You ain't even lookin'. Look at her."

"Yeah, he's all right, that Reinaldo," Gabi said.

"I see what you all lookin' at," Charlie said. He was holdin' a child by the hand. "I got me a partner better than his." He pointed at the little girl by his side. She must've been about four years old.

"Come on let's show'm," he said to her.

He started dancin'. The little girl followed. She knew the steps and kept time. She looked like a wind-up toy. People gathered round to watch Charlie dance with the baby. Other guys cut in, and the little girl kept dancin'. She'd dance with anyone.

"See that, they're all the same," Gabi said. "They're born that way."

When the music stopped, Reinaldo walked up to one of the mikes on the bandstand and welcomed everyone to the party. He made a short explanation of what El Pueblo was and asked the people for their support. It was a political speech, but I didn't know it when I heard it, 'cause it sounded like a guy askin' people to do somethin' that would be fun, like if the whole neighborhood was gonna plan a trip to Jones Beach. Reinaldo seemed like a guy who'd sit in front of *la bodega*, play dominoes and drink beer, you know, like if he grew up in the neighborhood, but latter Gabi told me he wasn't even a citizen. I don' know where Gabi got the information, but that's Gabi, always diggin' up info. Even if it wasn't true, that he wasn't a citizen, there must'a been a reason why people thought he wasn't. Nobody thought of it when he was makin' the speech. It was short. Everybody thought it was great.

Reinaldo got off the bandstand, and Flash took over. The music blared over the loudspeakers. Everyone grabbed a partner. The party was in full swing.

"Hello, Mario!" someone called to me.

It was Gladys Rivera. She lived next door to me, but she went to Catholic school. She could spell the longest word in English, and she was always tellin' people that she could do it. Personally, I didn't think that was anythin' to brag about. I can hit a Spalding the distance of three sewers, three and a half with the wind at my back, but I don' have to tell people. I just do it. You see, some things you just do, but other things you have to talk about, 'cause they're useless. There was things that Gladys didn' have to talk about. Other people did the talkin' for her. I'm not sayin' that I believe any of the gossip about Gladys. I used to have a very high opinion of her, not 'cause she could spell the longest word, you understand. She looked good in her uniform, her long blond hair fallin' over her shoulders. She was always laughing. Yeah, I used'ta think she was special until I saw her kissin' Papo. You might think that I was jealous, but that wasn't it, exactly. You see, this guy, Papo, was a bad sort. He lived down the block, but he wasn't like the rest of us. He was mean, and he'd been in reform school. Anyway I put her out of my mind after that.

"Hi," I responded.

"Isn't he great," she said.

"Who?"

"Reinaldo!"

"Yeah, he's all right."

We danced.

"I think he's adorable," she said.

"I wouldn't put it that way," I said.

Charlie danced over. He was in the arms of a fat woman, his aunt, a good dancer. We switched partners. Charlie's aunt could really cut it. Reinaldo was goin' around the lot rappin' to people. One thing about that guy, he could talk to anybody. His woman was just standin', lookin' impressive. Gabi was still watchin' Gloria dance with somebody else.

Somethin' hit me on my left shoulder. Somebody tryin' to be funny, I thought. I turned around, but I didn't discover the joker. A lotta of noise was comin' from the street. It looked like the party was movin' in that direction. There was a crashin' sound like garbage cans banged around, and things was flying through the air. A fight, I said to myself, rushing, like everyone else to get a look at the blood.

"Please go home, quickly! Go home before the police get here," Reinaldo's voice boomed over the loudspeaker.

I heard the sirens in the distance. I pushed my way through the crowd. There was a pile'a garbage in the middle of the street. People were bringin' more garbage and dumpin' it. Nobody was fightin'.

"What is this?" I asked.

"Go get some garbage!" shouted someone, wearin' an armband.

While Reinaldo was still in the crowd tellin' people to go home, the police arrived, and the people linked arms.

"Go home! Please go!"

A woman grabbed Reinaldo's arm. "Someone took my garbage can," she said. She pointed to a plastic can that had been left in the middle of the street.

He dashed in to get it. "Now go home!" he said as he handed it to her.

The first cop broke through the crowd and grabbed him.

"He wasn't the one! He wasn't the one!" the woman shouted.

Reinaldo pulled back, protestin' automatically. Another cop was on him. The first cop hit him with the nightstick. Reinaldo fought back, blood flowin' from his left eyebrow.

Now two cops were holdin' him. The first cop rammed the nightstick into his stomach. Reinaldo doubled over. The other cops were goin' through the crowd swingin' their nightsticks right and left. It was time to split.

I caught sight of Gabi. "Let's go!" I shouted.

"We gotta find Charlie!"

"He must be gone by now!"

"No, we gotta look."

"Come on! There he is"

Charlie was runnin' up the street ahead of us. We ran after him. As we ran, I noticed Gloria huddled in a doorway with some guy. Gabi didn't see them. I didn't say anythin'. When we got to the corner we saw John. Leanin' on a no parkin' sign, he was lookin' down the street to where the trouble was.

3

Sometimes you feel like there's no way out. You don' even know what from. Know what I mean? It's just this feeling like there's nothin', nothin' that makes any difference. When you feel good you're burstin' inside with somethin'; I don' know what. It's just a feelin', but when you have it, you don' need nothin' else. If you could have that feelin' all the time, then you could be happy, but it comes and goes. I thought maybe I could figure out how to get to feel like that or at least how to keep the feelin' when I got it, but it's no use.

Sometimes I feel great when I'm playin' stickball. I get caught up in the excitement of the game, you know specially when it's a close game and both teams are fightin' it out like their life depended on it. Every one on the team is givin' his excitement to every one else. Everybody's hooked up, so each person's energy is more. But it's not just the people; the whole area is charged, even the cars parked on the street. That's when you feel good, when you're connected to everythin', but how do you get that way? That's the question. It doesn't always happen when you play stickball. Sometimes you don' even feel like playin'. It's just a stupid game. You wish there was somethin' better to do. You might start to play in all seriousness, and the game turns into a goof. You start makin' ridiculous plays and everyone laughs. Pretty soon you got a circus on your hands. It's a bunch of clowns playing stickball. Sometimes that can be good—laughin' and horsin' around, but it's not the same as when you really get into the game. More often than not, the horsin' around leaves you with an empty feelin', drained, like an empty balloon.

Music and dancin' can get you connected too, specially dancin'. A whole room full of dancin' people, wow! Your whole body feels loose, and everybody looks good to you, even if you hated them yesterday, and you're gonna hate them tomorrow. It's that rhythm; your body flowin' with it makes somethin' happen. There is no stiffness between your soul and your body, between your body and everyone else. But even that is not a sure thing. You can get to the party and every part of you is like lead. Everythin' you hear sounds stupid. Every face you look at is deformed. It's like bein' alone in a booth made of one way mirrors. You can see everyone, but no one can see you; just as well, 'cause if they saw you, you might seem as disgustin' to them as they to you.

There's nothin' you can do about it. That's what really gets me. Sometimes you're somebody else, sort of; know what I mean? You can't decide feelings, like if somebody else was in charge. You even do things you don' wanna do or vise-versa. When I was a little kid I used to go to catechism class, and they gave you a whole list of things that were sins. So I decided I wanted to be good. I said to myself, I ain't never gonna do none of those things. It didn't do me no good to say that. It wasn't like I didn't try. Sometimes I try still, but you can't help doin' some of them things. It's nature; know what I mean? If you can't help it, how can it be a sin? That's what I wanna know.

It's puzzlin'. Take school for instance. That's where a lot of crazy things happen—specially when there's a substitute teacher, but even with regular teachers the place just drives you nutty. Last year some kids threw a desk out'a the third floor window. I never did nothin' like that, but I *have* thrown the wastepaper basket across the room. When you think about it, that's just as stupid. It could'a hurt somebody. I didn't wanna, but it could'a happened. I just had this urge to throw the basket. It bounced against the blackboard with a crash. It felt so good to hear the noise. Wammo! But right after I heard the basket hit the floor, and I felt good, the thought ran through my mind, "I could'a hit somebody." I imagined somebody's head split open, bleedin'. I got scared. I was almost tremblin'. Suddenly, Miss Markowitz, my history teacher, was standin' in front of me yellin'. It looked like her eyes were gonna pop right out of her head. Her whole face was distorted. Thinkin' back on it, I figure she probably was just as scared as I was, but I couldn't tell that then. At the moment she was ugly. Her face got all blotchy, and her green eyes went wild.

"You could've hurt someone," she shouted right at my face.

"I already know that," I said.

That made her more furious. I didn't mean anythin' other than what I said. I really knew it, and I was sorry.

"Don't get smart with me!" she screamed.

"Okay," I said. "I couldn't get smart even if I wanted to." I don' know why I said that, maybe 'cause I wasn't feelin' particularly smart at that moment. But then I never felt too smart in school.

"I'm losing my patience with you. What if I send you down to Mr. Frankel's office?"

"That ain't gonna do no good," I said.

Mr. Frankel was the assistant principal. I was tellin' the truth, though it might have sounded like I was afraid to go. I wasn't. I had been there often enough to know what an old fart he was. Still, I didn't wanna hassle. I wasn't scared really, but it was frustratin'. That's what it was. I would get a funny feelin' in my stomach, like it was churnin', then it would spread to the rest of my body, like if all my limbs were connected to my stomach by rubber bands stretched to their limit. I felt like they might snap any minute, and I would fall apart, in a heap, like a puppet. Sometimes I wished I would, once and for all.

Mr. Frankel looked like an ordinary human bein'. Well, maybe that's stretchin' it a bit. What I mean is that one would assume he was a human bein' despite his appearance. He was a funny lookin' dude, so serious too. He thought he looked sharp in his Orchard Street two-button suit. He wore a suit and tie every day, and he never took off his jacket. Even the principal sometimes walked around with shirtsleeves rolled up, but not Mr. Frankel. He was a suit and tie man all the way. He had a mat of brown hair and underneath it a dog's face. I'm not kiddin'. His fat cheeks hung down on both sides of his mouth like a St. Bernard. Maybe if I had been talkin' to a dog, he would'a understood me better than Mr. Frankel did. He didn't understand anythin'—like the time they caught me writin' on the wall.

"You here again," he said from behind his desk.

"Yeah,"

"Why were you writing on the wall? What possible satisfaction can you get out of defacing the school?" he asked.

I wasn't sure if he was talkin' to me or to himself, but I guess it was to me 'cause then he looked straight at my nose and asked again, "Why?"

"I don' know," I said.

"You don't know," he always repeated what other people said.

"I got the urge," I tried to explain.

"You got the urge," he repeated.

"Yeah," I said, "I couldn't help it. Sometimes you get the urge to be famous."

"To be famous?" he seemed surprised. "That's the most ridiculous thing I ever heard. A man," he said pulling himself up as if to show what a man was, "obtains fame by performing constructive acts."

"Art is constructive," I said.

“What does art have to do with it?”

“I didn’t just write my name on the wall; I drew it.”

“By no stretch of the imagination, young man,” he stood up and spoke louder, “can an act of vandalism be transformed into art. Any redeeming social value of your writing on the wall escapes me entirely.”

What the hell was he talkin’ about? I didn’t understand a word. To me, the matter was simple. I don’ know why it wasn’t obvious to him. Everybody wants to be known, so you write your name on the wall, right? So even when you’re not there it’s like sayin’ hello to everyone who comes by. It’s like walkin’ down the street and bein’ able to greet everyone, right? It makes you feel good. If you’re in a strange place, there’s a wall between you and everythin’ else, that’s nowhere. It’s the same with the names. You look at all these brightly colored letters. They’re sayin’ hello. So you don’ have to feel like a stranger anymore. That’s simple. I don’ know why Mr. Frankel didn’t see it that way.

Still, I could see that his head was somewhere else, if you know what I mean? He was into the wall. I tried to reach him from a different angle.

“It’s only a wall,” I said.

“It’s only a wall!” he exclaimed.

I knew right then, from the expression on his face, that it was no use tryin’ to get’m around to a reasonable point of view. He was obsessed with a two-tone wall.

So I was suspended for a week, and I had to scrub my name off the wall, except that it wouldn’t come off. I only managed to make it look faded. It was ridiculous—tryin’ ta rub the spray paint off a wall—beside it was an improvement, the graffiti I mean. But there's no arguin' with some people.

Now you see why I didn't wanna go see Mr. Frankel. It would lead to more trouble. I would try to explain to him why I threw the wastebasket, but he wouldn't'a listened. That's the problem with people like that. They think they already know everythin', so they don' listen to others. I thought that I'd have a much better chance of explainin' it to Miss Markowitz. Not that she was any great listener herself, but it was sometimes possible to get through to her, though there seemed to be no rhyme or reason as to when she would be understandin' and when not. She was a little bit insane—like in this movie I saw on TV, where a woman is three different people in one. Each personality didn't have any control over what the others did. You know maybe we're all a little bit like that! Me too. I tried to explain that to her.

"You're not different from me," I said.

"I beg your pardon," said she.

"You know somethin'," I said, "you got a split personality."

She boiled over.

"I don't need this," she hissed. "I don't need this."

What the hell was that about? I didn't need it either, but that's the way it is, you know? She was gettin' angrier and angrier.

"Get in your seat," she shouted.

"Let me explain," I pleaded. "I didn't wanna throw the trashcan. Somethin' made me do it."

"What?" she screamed at the top of her lungs. "What made you do it?"

"The devil made him do it," someone said from the back of the room. The whole class cracked up. I knew I didn't have a chance then.

"Get in your seat and stay there," she screamed at me.

I figured I better do it. I didn't have to go to Mr. Frankel's office, and there was no use tryin' to educate Miss Markowitz while she was so angry. She was beside herself, you might say.

Well, you see that's the way it is. In school the teacher always misses the point. Take for instance when I get interested in somethin', 'cause I ain't always throwing things around. Sometimes I get involved. Boy, I work like a maniac. It don' last very long, but everybody notices. The teacher comes over to me and says, "You see, you can do it when you try." I say, "I wasn't tryin'." Then she looks at me with disbelief, like she doesn't understand what I'm talkin' about. I guess she thinks that all the other times I just don' wanna be learnin', but that ain't so. I was tryin' but not gettin' anywhere. I don' know why. Then somethin' happened. I wasn't tryin' any harder. I just got interested. Well that's the way it is. You see the problem? In real life when you're not interested in somethin', you go on to somethin' else, right? Like if you don' wanna hang around the block and play ball, you can get together with the guys and go to the beach or somethin'. But in school you got to sit there, whether you're interested or not. It's torture. And you know what torture can do to a guy, right? Drive him batty. Personally, I think that's what happened to Charlie. Maybe it wasn't just school, but school had a lot to do with it.

If you saw Charlie in school you'd think that he was a mental case. Now that's different from plain crazy, sort of. See, when I said before that Charlie was crazy that was more like sayin' he didn't use his head, know what I mean—a little stupid. When I say he's a mental case, that's a whole other ball game. Mental case is when you're ready for the straight jacket, the institution. First of all, Charlie wore a hat all the time. That hat was to Charlie as a suit was to Mr. Frankel, if you know what I mean. You might think that wearin' a hat all the time is not so strange, and it isn't, if you're normal. But with Charlie it was more. You've heard of little kids that have a blanket or maybe a teddy bear or a doll that they always hang on to, and if you take it away from them they go berserk or into shock or somethin'. Well, that's the way Charlie was about his hat. One day Mr. Lipshitz, the gym teacher, tried to make him take it off. Boy, what a scene that was! Now imagine Mr. Lipshitz, a baldheaded ape in a t-shirt, hair around his ears, but the top of his head looked like it was shellacked more than the gym floor.

"Mr. Soto," said Mr. Lipshitz, speakin' to Charlie, "gentlemen do not wear hats indoors."

"Good for them," said Charlie. "That ain't got nothin' to do with me."

"I don't think you get my meaning Mr. Soto."

"I don' think I do," Charlie said.

This wasn't happenin' in the gym, but in the hall, so Charlie probably felt he didn't have to take Mr. Lipshitz all that seriously, especially with Mr. Lipshitz callin' him Mr. and all. You know how gym teachers get to think like they're in the army or somethin'. They begin to act like in those movies about military schools, where everybody calls everybody else "Mr."

"Take off your hat Mr. Soto."

Charlie's face got dark for a moment. The joke was goin' too far, and the only thing he could do was take it a little further.

"What hat?" he asked, tryin' to smile.

"Take off your hat Mr. Soto."

I could see that somethin' was gonna happen. Mr. Lipshitz was too stupid to realize it. He wasn't callin' the shots on this one. The corners of Charlie's mouth were twitchin' slightly—hardly noticeable, but I was used to watchin' Charlie's face. His eyes too were beginnin' to go. They would become fixed, like if they was lookin' at nothin'. I was tryin' to figure what I could do, when Mr. Lipshitz grabbed the hat. That was it.

I don' know exactly what happened next, but Charlie was on Mr. Lipshitz. I got pushed aside by the crowd that suddenly gathered. Next thing I saw was Gabi holdin' Charlie against the wall tryin' to calm him down. Charlie had a stickball bat in his hand. Someone in the crowd must'a passed it to him.

"Take it easy," Gabi was sayin'. "Take it easy."

"Motherfucker took my hat," Charlie screamed. "Ain't nobody gonna take my hat."

His face was all red. His eyes had widened and looked fierce. Teachers had come out of their rooms and were tryin' to disperse the crowd.

"Kill that motherfucker," someone said to Charlie.

Charlie stared at the person as if he hadn't understood what he'd said.

"Come on take it easy, Charlie," Gabi kept sayin'.

"My hat, gimme my hat," his face was beginnin' to soften. Then he started to cry. There he was, big tough Charlie cryin'. I would'n'a believed it if I hadn't seen it with my own eyes.

Anyway, he was only suspended for a little while. I guess he was lucky Gabi got there so quick and grabbed him before he could really hurt Mr. Lipshitz, else Charlie would'a been in real trouble. Gabi was always doin' that, you know—protectin' Charlie. A lot'a times he would calm him down, or he would talk for him to teachers, like if he was Charlie's lawyer. I suppose that's what you call a real friend, and Charlie needed one, though I don' know what he ever did for Gabi. I guess they was more like brothers than friends, 'cause you do things for your brother even though he might not be able to do nothin' for you. Like I said, Charlie really needed a friend, 'specially in school. Usually, when you saw him in class, which wasn't very often, he was freaked out. He would beat on the desk like if it was a bongo drum. There was no way to get him to stop, 'cause he would look at you like you was crazy to want him to stop. Teachers would try to ignore him mostly. That was hard, 'cause sometimes the drummin' got contagious, so everyone around Charlie would start bangin' away and keep on until they got tired. Except Charlie, he never got tired. Of course, other times he was a different person altogether. He would be quiet. He would sit by the window and watch whatever was goin' on in the street, as if he was seriously thinkin' about life. Teachers didn't like that either, 'cause obviously he wasn't payin' attention, but at least it was better than his bongo playin'.

When you're in a school full of Charlies you're glad when summer vacation rolls around. Except that more and more every other person on the street is just as nutty. It's like the whole world is going crazy. All you read about in the paper is crimes. The other day, I read about two little kids who set fire to a warehouse just for kicks. Then there's all the things that never get reported, specially things that happen around here. Enough things happen on this block to fill up a whole newspaper. Imagine if everythin' was reported. There wouldn't be enough paper to print it on. It's not that the police don' know about it. As a matter of fact a lot'a times they're involved, you know what I mean? Like I used to think that gamblin' was illegal, right? So I always saw these guys rollin' dice, right out on the street too, and I wondered how come they didn't worry that cops would come around and bust up the game. I kept an eye on them, 'cause sooner or later the cops might show up. When a squad car pulled around the corner, I said to myself, "Those guys are gonna scram now." Wrong, they kept on playin'—didn't even hide the mula, right there on the sidewalk piles of it. Cops pulled up to the curb, a white cop and a black one. The white cop gets out of the car, walks over to the crap game. He put his hand on the shoulder of one of the guys. The guy turns around and smiles. He's a big guy. The cop smiles back. They talk a little. Some of the other guys talk and everybody laughs. The big guy counts out some money, gives it to the cop. The cop walks back to the car, gets in, drives away. Happened right out in the open, and I was watchin'. That ain't so bad, right? A cop is like everybody else, gotta make a little on the side. Three days later there was a fight over a game and a man got stabbed. Ambulance came, squad car came, the man was taken to the hospital, but nobody was arrested. Well, that's the way it is. And how about the pushers? How come they don' get arrested? But that's a whole other story; ain't nothin' I can do about it. The whole world is crazy. You gotta be cool—keep your wits about you, else you're a goner. Me, I walk straight ahead, don' turn my head for nothin'. I just catch everythin' out of the corner of my eyes. Maybe I'll make it, and maybe I won't, but the devil is gonna have to run hard to catch me.

4

As I was sayin', sometimes you get to feel like a coca-cola gone flat, and you don' know why. I was feelin' that way the Monday after the block party. I went out and sat on the stoop to wait for Gabi and Charlie to show up. We never made no agreement to meet, but we sort'a got into the habit. I went down early. It wasn't too hot yet, but I could tell it was gonna be one of those uncomfortable days. After a while, Gabi showed up without Charlie.

"Where is Charlie?" I asked.

"I don' know," Gabi said, "I went to his house, but nobody was home."

"Not even his grandmother?"

"Nobody."

"Maybe she was home alone and was afraid to answer the door."

"Maybe, but where's Charlie?"

"I don' know," I said. "He ain't been here."

"Maybe he's playin' handball," Gabi said. "Let's go check."

We went down to the handball courts, but he wasn't there. Andy Coto and some other guys were hangin' out by the checker tables. Andy was a ladies' man, if you know what I mean, good stickball player, too. But he was a klepto. I ain't got nothin' against stealin'. Everybody steals, but Andy, he stole even when he didn't wanna. Like he would steal somethin', and he wouldn't even know it. Now, that's sick!

"You guys wanna get a game together?" he asked.

"Nah, we're lookin' for Charlie. You seen'm?"

"Yeah, saw'm with this baldheaded guy givin' out some handbills.

"What about?"

"Somethin' about a meetin'—somethin' about police horribleness some shit like that."

"You got one?"

"Nah, I don' mess with that shit."

"You know where he is now?"

"Beats me," Andy said.

There was only one place to look for him now, so we headed towards Lexin'ton Avenue. When we got to the storefront, Reinaldo's girlfriend was the only person there. Well, that brightened up my day considerably, if you know what I mean. She wasn't so stunnin' like at the block party. She wasn't dressed fancy or anythin', but I had in my mind that picture of her in a long dress dancin' across the bright lights. There was somethin' about her that made everythin' else around disappear. It wasn't that she was stacked or anythin' like that. I mean she wasn't bad lookin', but she wasn't no pin-up girl either. It was somethin' else—physical but not describable, you wouldn't see it in no photograph. Or you might, but it would be an accident or a trick. One thing I learned: you can't trust a camera. Sometimes from a photograph you think that a person has soul, but then you meet them in person and it's not there. You see, it was a trick. You can do that with a camera. Or the opposite can happen. Somebody can look flat in a picture, and you knowin' perfectly well that's not the way it is for real. Some people believe that the camera always tells the truth, that it's the human eye that makes mistakes. But that's ridiculous. Of course, I know eyes can make mistakes, but cameras can make lies. I'd rather trust my own eyes. I saw this television show about people who wanted ta settle whether a castle was haunted, so they tried to take pictures of the ghosts. Well naturally there weren't any ghosts in the photos, 'cause some things can be seen only by the naked eye.

"We're lookin' for Charlie," Gabi explained.

"He's out distributing leaflets," she said.

"By himself?" Gabi asked. That's how cagey Gabi can be. He already knew that Charlie wasn't by himself, but he wanted to be cool, know what I mean? So I figured Gabi didn't trust Michelle.

"No, he's not alone," she said. He's with John. We're organizing a meeting, and we're going from house to house giving out the leaflets. You guys want to help?"

"Not me," Gabi said. "I gotta find Charlie."

"I'll stay," I said. "See you later Gabi."

"Okay," Gabi said. He looked at me, but he didn't ask me to go with him.

5

I didn't understand Michelle. I didn't understand what she was doin' in El Barrio. She wasn't a social worker. She was too nice for that. She could'a been right out of a Dick and Jane book, right? Remember them books? A policeman is a friendly guy who directs traffic and tells you how to get home when you get lost. El Barrio is not Dick and Jane country, and there she was. What was she, just Reinaldo's girlfriend?

I asked her, "How did you meet Reinaldo?"

"In school," she answered.

That threw me for a loop. He was much older than she, so how could they be in school together. Then I thought he was her teacher. No, I said to myself, Reinaldo a teacher? Impossible! How could that be? My face must'a shown what was goin' through my mind, 'cause she said: "I had him for a theater course in college."

"He was a professor?"

"For that year," she said.

"If that don' beat all!"

"You're surprised?"

"Sure, he just don' seem like a professor."

"He's remarkable," she said.

"Yeah, what did he teach?"

"Acting."

"You was learnin' to be an actress? For the Movies?"

"No," she said, "just for fun."

"So Reinaldo was your teacher. I would'a never guessed, you know. Don' he look just like an ordinary guy, just hustlin' to get along? I don' mean ordinary in any old way; I mean he doesn't give himself airs. He don' got an attitude like you would think a professor would. You know what I mean? He hangs around with all these uneducated people, and you would never know that he was any different from them."

"He's written books, too."

"Yeah, what kind'a books?"

"Novels and stories. They've been published in South America."

We kept on talkin' about Reinaldo for a while. She told me that he'd been married, that he had a child, that he'd worked in an advertisin' agency, and he'd been makin' lots'a money.

He was makin' a lot of money, and he left to hang around here? This was gettin' puzzlin'. My first reaction to him had been right—he was crazy.

"What did he used to do in advertisin'?" I asked.

"He was a copywriter."

"What's that?"

"He would write the words for advertisements, for commercials."

"Well, that doesn't sound like a hard job for somebody who can write books," I said.

"It wasn't a hard job in that sense."

"So why did he leave?"

"It wasn't the kind of life he wanted."

"He'd rather be poor?"

"There are more important things to be done in the world than trying to brainwash people into buying one kind of soap instead of another."

"I can't write for beans," I said, " but if I could, I wouldn't mind a job like that—make money, move to a nice place, good clothes, car, you know. I wouldn't mind that at all."

"Yes," she said, "one man's meat is another man's poison."

I don' think that she was too happy with what I was sayin'. Her face changed. It was very noticeable like turnin' out a light. That's not what I wanted to do.

"Yeah, it takes all kinds," I said. But I was still curious about Reinaldo. "Did he live around here when he had money?" I asked.

"No, he lived in Long Island," she said automatically as if she was somewhere else.

"They have nice houses there, don' they?"

"Yes," she said. "His wife still lives there."

"His wife? He's still married?"

"No," she said, "he's divorced."

It was time to change the subject. "What about you? Where do you come from," I asked.

"From the Bronx," she answered. "We better get going," she continued and handed me a stack a leaflets, then took a stack for herself. "You lead the way. We'll give them out on your block," she said.

"If we give them to people on the street, they're just gonna throw them away," I said.

"No, we'll knock on doors. That way we'll get to talk to people."

"That ain't gonna work either," I said. "People ain't gonna open their doors."

"Well, let's try."

We went to the top floor of a buildin' and started to work our way down. The first three doors we knocked on there was no answer.

"Why don' we put the leaflets on the door knobs and leave," I said. "That'll save a lotta time. We'll cover more ground."

"No, that's not as effective."

We knocked on another door. A voice from inside softly asked, "Welfare?"

"No," Michelle answered, "we're from El Barrio, a community organization. May we speak with you for a minute..."

The woman attached the chain lock and unbolted the door.

"Welfare?" she asked again.

Apparently she'd not understood what Michelle had said. The woman was young. She had a very thin face and large eyes. She looked puzzled to see strangers at the door who were not from the welfare department. A very small child squeezed passed her and looked up at us through the slightly opened door. The child was half dressed and suckin' on a pacifier.

I explained in Spanish what Michelle had said. The woman smiled faintly as she led us into the apartment. The livin' room was dark. Its only window faced a brick wall. The room was painted psychedelic blue, with all the doorframes and moldin' dark brown. It was an ordinary apartment, but I watched Michelle as she took it all in. I could tell it was strange to her. The furniture in bad shape, but after all, what can you expect to buy with a welfare check. Still, there was a mirror over the sofa that looked new, but I think mirrors always look that way if they're clean. A lot'a people had mirrors like that in their livin' rooms. I guess somethin' becomes a style when all the furniture stores push it, and like you could see this mirror in all the store windows. It was rectangular with the edges at an angle to form a frame about four inches wide all around. On the lower left hand corner was painted a branch of a tree extendin' over water and on the branch a leopard. Now this mirror was fascinatin' to me, and I could look at it for hours. At one time, I thought the whole mirror was supposed to represent the water. I hadn't thought of that when I first looked at it, and I was amazed when I realized it. That was clever. But that wasn't the only thing I liked about the mirror. What I liked best was that it was hot and cold. You see the leopard was brightly painted. It's a jungle animal, and jungles are hot places, but the glass reminded me of ice. The mixture created a strange feeling in me.

Michelle explained to the woman what El Pueblo was and told her what happened at the block party. I translated.

"The police must know what they're doin'," the woman said. "After all, we have enough garbage in the street without people throwin' more."

"Tell her that the police have no right to beat people," Michelle said. "How can they tell who's guilty and who's innocent? That's for the court to decide."

"Some people have to be beaten, else they don't learn," the woman said.

"Ask her if she'd been there and had been hurt by the cops whether she would think it was fair."

"I wouldn't have got involved," the woman said. "I stay out of trouble."

The child began to tug at her skirt, and she pushed him aside. He dropped the pacifier and started to cry. The mother picked up the pacifier, wiped it, stuck it back in the baby's mouth.

"Don't you want to live in a better place, eat better food, get the best for your baby?" Michelle kept on.

"Life is uncertain. We have to bear whatever God sends," she answered. "Some people think that by asking for trouble life will get better. But no, that only makes it worse."

"Come to the meeting tonight," Michelle said. She sounded exhausted. "The address is right here on this paper," she handed a leaflet to the woman.

"I'll try," the woman answered.

Out in the hallway I felt sorry for Michelle. "It's gonna be this way all over," I said. "There's no talkin' to people—about this anyway. In fact I don' understand it myself. Why is it so important to you?"

"It's important for everyone," she said.

"You think that woman is gonna come to the meetin'? She's not."

"Maybe she will."

One flight down we knocked on another door. No answer. We knocked next door. A girl, half her hair in rollers, came to the door.

"Well, there's nobody here but me, so you can't talk to anybody," she said after we explained what we wanted.

"How about you?" Michelle asked.

"I'm settin' my hair. I don't have time."

"Anyway take this, and come to the meeting tonight." Michelle gave her a leaflet.

After that we got rid of the leaflets as fast as we could by slippin' them under doors or leavin' them on doorknobs. All the ones left, we gave out in the street.

6

When I saw Gabi again, he told me he hadn't found Charlie all day. We couldn't figure where he could possibly be.

"I'm gonna go by his house again and see if he's there. You wanna come?"

"Okay," I said, and followed him out to the street.

"We'll take the shortcut across the 105th Street lot," Gabi said.

When we got to 105th Street, we went down into a basement and through a backyard. A dog started to bark ferociously and paw at some door. My heart almost came out of my mouth. I've always been scared'a dogs. We had to climb a wire fence. Gabi made it over before me. I was so nervous I could hardly grip the mesh; my foot kept slippin'.

"Hey, you shittin' green up there?" Gabi said.

"Fuck you," I answered.

Half way down the other side of the fence I jumped, almost twisted my ankle.

"You okay?" Gabi asked.

"Yeah, I'm all right," I said.

We started across the empty lot watchin' to step carefully, 'cause the lot was full of garbage. We didn't wanna step on no broken bottles or rusty nails. We got through the lot and we had to go through another basement to get to the street. This time we didn't have to climb. There was a hole in the fence.

"Hey, there's someone in there," Gabi said.

In the darkness we could see a bulky figure.

"It's a guy," I said.

"I know it's a guy."

"Let's wait here til' he goes."

The figure was carryin' somethin' in each hand. He was goin' out to the street. We followed at a safe distance. Even in the street, it was too dark to make out who he was. In any case, we didn't care who it was. We just didn't wanna run into no burglar.

"You know, that outline looks kind of familiar," Gabi said.

The figure passed under a streetlight, and we saw him clearly. It was Charlie. We ran after him shoutin' his name. He was startled and almost took off before he realized it was us.

"Man, where you been all day?" Gabi asked.

"Just hangin' out," he answered.

"We been lookin' for you all over."

"Well, you found me."

"You could'a let us know where you was gonna be."

I smelled gasoline.

"You been hangin' out in a gas station?" I asked.

"Listen you guys, I can't tell you anythin'. I promised. I always keep my promises," he said.

"You got gasoline in those cans?" Gabi asked.

"Don't ask me, man. I can't tell you."

"I can smell it. I know it's gasoline. Where are you goin' with it?"

"Up the block. That's all."

"You know you could get in trouble carryin' gasoline around. What if some cops see you? They might think you're some kind of maniac. They'd take you in for sure"

"Ain't no cops gonna catch me man, if I hurry up and take these cans where I'm suppose to. If you're so worried stop babblin'."

"Where you goin' with them?"

"They're for John. I'm takin'm to El Pueblo."

"For John? What the hell is he gonna do with gasoline. He don' even have a car."

"He wants to make some firebombs, man. He wants to burn down some schools."

"You're crazy! Let's throw away the cans and go home."

"I can't. I promised."

"Well, you can't walk in the street like this. You'll get caught."

"There's no other way, man," Charlie said.

"This is what we'll do," Gabi said. "I'll walk a block ahead of you, and Mario a block behind. If we see any cops, we'll give you a signal, and you hide the cans."

We all agreed on that. Gabi went up ahead, and I stayed behind. I was scared. My stomach felt like I'd swallowed a kitten. We walked that way for a few blocks till we got to 101st Street, then Gabi stopped. My knees began to shake. Gabi turned around and gave Charlie the signal. Charlie put the gasoline cans down between some trash piled on the side of a buildin'. They both walked back to where I was.

"What's the matter?" I asked.

"Cops," Gabi answered. "They're parked on 101st. Three squad cars, like if they was waitin' for somethin'."

"It's a trap," I said.

"We gotta do somethin'," Charlie said. "We gotta warn those guys."

"We can't, man. It's too late. We'll be caught with them."

"We gotta do somethin'," he repeated.

"Let's get out'a of here," I said.

"Let's wait a while and see what happens," Gabi said. "We're safe here. Anyway, now that John doesn't have any gasoline there won't be any evidence."

"No, man," Charlie said, "somebody else was bringin' gasolin' too."

We waited for a while and nothin' happened. We got tired, so we sat on a stoop. Every once in a while one of us would get up and look to see if anythin' was happenin'. The waiting felt like it was forever.

"Nothin's gonna happen," I said.

"Maybe not," Gabi said. "Let's give it a few more minutes."

We waited some more, then we started to walk back uptown.

"Maybe we should go right up to those cops and ask'm what they're waitin' for," Charlie said.

Suddenly, we heard sirens all over the place. We turned to see the cop cars roundin' the corner towards El Pueblo, sirens full blast and lights flashin'. One of the squad cars turned in our direction.

"Run for it," Gabi shouted. His voice almost cracked.

Charlie and me, we followed Gabi. He went into a buildin' and started runnin' up the stairs. I looked behind me. Charlie had dropped his hat, and he was goin' back for it.

"Leave the fuck'n hat," I shouted at him.

He didn't pay no attention to me. Gabi had stopped on the landin' above.

"Jesus Christ, Charlie you're crazy; leave the hat."

Charlie snatched up the hat from the floor, and we continued up the stairs. We weren't sure whether anyone was followin' us, but we wasn't about to stop and find out. We got to the roof and listened. Someone was comin' up the stairs.

"They're not even runnin'," I said.

"Those fuck'n cops are too fat to run," Gabi said. "We gotta get off this roof."

We walked around the edge of the roof, and then we realized we were in trouble. We couldn't just walk on to the next roof. The buildin' on one side was bein' demolished. It had no roof. On the other side there was a gap between the next roof and us.

"We're gonna have to jump," Gabi said.

"Hell no!" I said. "That's too far. We'll never make it."

"It's either that or get caught."

"I'm for jumpin'," Charlie said. "I can jump that easy. I've been in trainin', you know." Charlie was overweight. "Who's goin' first?"

"I'll go," Gabi said.

There was no railin' on this roof. Gabi took a runnin' start and jumped. He made it.

"It's your turn now Mario," Charlie said.

"You go first," I said to Charlie.

"No sir, age before beauty," he said.

"Will you guys stop horsin' around and hurry up," Gabi shouted.

"Come on, Mario, go already!" Charlie insisted.

I thought of all my bones bein' crushed as I hit the cement five stories below. That's not the way I wanted to die. I imagined the pain. I know I'm a coward deep down inside, but I don' think anybody is braver, really. I think everybody gets scared. Those who don't, they're the crazy ones. So I made the sign of the cross and I jumped. A split second later I was standin' next to Gabi. Only, my heart was beatin' so fast, I thought I might get a heart attack.

"Okay, Charlie, hurry up," Gabi shouted at him.

"Here I come," Charlie said.

He went back a ways and ran towards the edge, but he slowed down and stopped.

"You think he can make it?" I asked Gabi.

"Sure, he can make it."

I trusted Gabi to know enough about Charlie, so if Gabi was sure, I took it for granted that Charlie could do it.

Charlie walked back to the startin' point, and took another runnin' start. He was about to leap when the police arrived on the roof. "Stop!" one of them shouted.

Charlie lost his balance. When he hit the ground it was like a gunshot.

I took hold of Gabi. He looked terrible, like the flesh was gonna melt right off his face, tremblin' all over.

"Come on Gabi, we gotta get out of here."

The cops wasn't takin' any chances in tryin' to jump over to our roof, and I knew it was too dark for them to have gotten a good look at us. We could still get away.

"We can't leave Charlie, we can't! We gotta help him."

"Ain't nothin' we can do. The cops will call an ambulance. That's all anybody can do. It ain't no use us gettin' caught too," I said.

I put my arm around him and dragged him. He didn't have the strength to resist. He was almost limp. We went over a couple of roofs and then down to the street. There was a lot of people on the street now, tryin' to find out what was happenin'. I figured the best thing to do was to go back to Andy Coto's basement. There wasn't no use taking Gabi home in his condition. His mother would hassle him some more and make things worse. I figured there wasn't no sense in me goin' home either. I just wasn't up to it. Anyway, in the street I was scared shitless. I thought any minute a bunch of cops would fall on us, but as it turned out it seemed like they wasn't even lookin' for us. Even if a squad car passed by they would'a thought we was a couple of winos stumblin' down the street. That's what we must'a looked like—me with my arm around Gabi and him fallin' apart.

When we got there, I took Gabi right into the apartment, and sat'm down. Then I went outside to fetch Andy. He came back in with me. Raymond Cazzario did too.

"This is bad, man," Andy said. "This is bad."

I agreed.

"Hey, Gabi, you gonna be all right," Andy said. He had a very cool and detached way of bein' concerned.

"Yeah, man, he's gonna be all right," I said.

"I'm okay," he said.

He was shiverin', but it must'a been ninety degrees in the room.

"Get a blanket and cover him," Raymond said.

"Cover him? It's hot as hell," Andy said. Brains wasn't his department.

"Hey, man, you're suppose'ta do that," Raymond said. "Don' you see the guy is in shock? Jesus, some people don' know nothin'."

"I'm all right," Gabi said.

Andy went to look for a blanket. I could see Gabi wasn't all right at all. He started to throw up. I took him into the bathroom. I thought his guts was gonna come out. I breathed through my mouth. I didn't wanna start throwin' up too.

7

The next day I was so wiped out I could hardly stay on

my feet. I was depressed. Charlie's fallin' off the roof was on my mind, and at the same time it wasn't. He had fallen, but I didn't really realize that he could be dead, or hurt or in a lot of pain. Like his fallin' didn't connect with any of the results. It wasn't like I was tryin' not to think about it. I thought about it, but it was just like nothin'. I got to thinkin' whether people would say I was coldhearted and without feelings. I wasn't sure whether it was good to be that way or not. I guess in some ways it's good, 'cause terrible things are always happening, you know, and you can't be falling to pieces all the time, 'cause that's nowhere, right? But certain times people expect you to show your feelings, and if you don't, they get the wrong idea; you know what I mean? Like if you don't cry at a funeral, they're gonna say you didn't care about the dead person. That don't have to be true at all. Sometimes a person gets the habit of not having feelings, 'cause feelings is what hurts you, know what I mean? Like sometimes you have a feelings inside, like your chest is gonna split open, crack in two, and you know it's 'cause your feelings is hurt. That pain is too much, like if you love somebody that don' love you back. When you're hurtin', you might look at a tree or a rock and you think, that tree and that rock don' have no problems with feelings. You wish you could be like that, you know what I mean? Like, sometimes I wish everyone could just have a brain with no feelings, just reason then there wouldn't be no problems in the world. That's what I think.

You see, when God made people he made them in a funny way. He made them so that sometimes they would be smart and sometimes not. I don' know what he had in mind when he did that. Like if you wash the white stuff and color stuff in the same water everything is gonna get messed up, right? So if you put the logic and the feelings in the same box, on a bumpy road everythin's gonna get tangled up. I just don't understand it. For instance, sometimes you do something that you think is smart, the later you realize what you did was stupid. It was your feelings getting in the way. There's just no way to keep the two apart.

Anyway, like I said before, sometimes you manage to put your feelings away somewhere so that you wouldn't be gettin' hurt all the time, but sometimes when you want them to come out, they just don't. They forgot the way back. Sometimes I think there's just no way to win in this world. I didn't know whether Charlie was dead or alive, and I couldn't get into thinkin' about it, though I figured he must be dead. Gabi was still sleepin' and Andy had gone out to get somethin' to eat. I wasn't hungry myself. I felt like I had a hangover. I went to the kitchen lookin' for some orange juice. The refrigerator was almost empty—three beer cans, a container of milk and some moldy cheese. I opened the freezer, and found a can of Minute Maid, but then I couldn't find what to mix it in, no pitcher, no bowl, I decided to use a cookin' pot, what the hell, right? I was tryin' to get the lump of frozen juice to dissolve in the water when Andy came back with a bag of groceries.

"I brought a friend of yours," he said. "Come in here," he called to someone in the livin' room.

It was Michelle. She looked like she'd been cryin'.

"Hi," I said. "What are you doing here?"

"I met Andy on the street. He said you were here, so I came to see if you're okay."

"I'm okay," I said, "until the cops catch up with me. I didn't even have anythin' to do with them guys, and now I'm in a mess."

"You'll be all right," she said. "They're not interested in you. The whole thing was set up to get Reinaldo and Flash."

"And John was in on it?"

"It seems that way."

"That motherfucker! I knew he was up to somethin'."

"You know anythin' about Charlie?" Andy asked.

"He's dead," she answered. I thought she might start cryin' again, but she controlled herself.

"Flash and Reinaldo are in jail?"

"They got Flash. Reinaldo escaped. He's leaving the country."

"Where will he go?" I asked.

"I don't know," she said. "I think he's going home to join the guerrillas in his own country."

We heard Gabi gettin' up in the bedroom.

"We gotta tell him about Charlie," Andy said.

"Don' tell him nothin' unless he asks," I said.

Gabi came in lookin' like he was sleepwalkin'.

"You want some breakfast?" Andy asked.

"Jesus, I ain't hungry," he said.

"Here, have some orange juice," I said. I poured some orange juice into a cup and gave it to'm.

"I guess I gotta get home," he said in a dreamy sort of voice.

"Yeah, me too," I said.

"I'll walk you over," Michelle said. I guess she didn't

wanna be alone. I didn't understand why she wasn't with Reinaldo, less he had left already. First I thought she should'a gone with him, but then I figured he was a crazy person, and there wasn't no sense in her being crazy too. I figured he was gonna get killed sooner or later, so there wasn't no use in her followin' anyway.

"See you around, Andy," I said, "and thanks. I really mean it."

"Anytime," he said.

We was out in the street walkin' home, and I realized that when I got there I was gonna be depressed.

"You know somethin'?" I said. "I don' wanna go home."

"Me neither, I guess," Gabi said.

"Let's go to Coney Island," I said.

"That's too fuck'n far," he said.

"No it ain't. You wanna go to Coney Island?" I asked Michelle.

"It's okay with me," she answered.

"That's a fuck'n long ride on the subway," Gabi said.

"Come on it'll be fun. It's always fun in the subway."

"Jesus Christ! You have a fucked up sense of fun."

We walked towards the subway. All this time Gabi hadn't said nothing about Charlie. After we was in the subway for a while, I really got to thinking that it was a long way to Coney Island. "This is a fuck'n long ride," I said.

"Jesus Christ!" Gabi said lookin' at me like if I had insulted him or somethin'. "You ain't gonna back out now, shit!"

"Hell no," I said, and I started to laugh. I didn't know

where that laugh came from, 'cause I was feeling shitty, if you know what I mean. But it was like this heavy thing inside my chest split open, and the laughter just popped out. It kind'a had a rough time gettin' through my throat, the laughter I mean. It wasn't easy, but I couldn't help it. I looked at Gabi's face, and it made me laugh. I looked at the other people in the car, and they made me laugh too. Everybody started lookin' at me, you know, all the other people in the car, and that made me laugh all the more.

"Why's everybody lookin' this way?"

"You're makin' a fool of yourself," Gabi said. "Sit quiet and behave. Jesus, you're gonna embarrass Michelle."

I looked at Michelle. She didn't seem embarrassed, but I couldn't help laughin' at her. As I watched her, I became very sad. Really, I was sad all along; I don' really know what was happenin'. As I watched Michelle, she began to change. No, that's not exactly right either. She was still Michelle. She was and she wasn't. I didn't feel like laughin' anymore. I had a strange sensation that Michelle was takin' us somewhere for some unknown reason, although I knew we was goin' to Coney Island, and that it had been my idea to go there.

Anyway, that sobered me up. I vaguely heard Michelle say, "Take it easy, Mario." The three of us sat there quietly, but after a couple of stops, I began to stare at the lady sittin' across from me. She noticed that I was lookin' at her, and she looked away. She was too uncomfortable to look back at me. Every once in a while she would check to see if I was still starin' at her. I kept right on, and she began to fidget. She was an older woman. Her wrinkled eyes was sunk in her pudgy face. I started to giggle. I had an uncontrollable desire to laugh louder. To my surprise Michelle also began to giggle. She was tryin' to keep it in check, but she couldn't. She burst out as loud as me. Panic covered the woman's face. She got up and moved to the other end of the car.

"Jesus Christ, both of yous are crazy," Gabi said.

"I ain't crazy," I said between chuckles.

"You're both loony," he said. "I don' wanna be seen with either one of you."

He got up and walked to the next car.

"Hey, Gabi, come back," I called.

"Don' be like that, Gabi," Michelle said.

We followed him.

"Stop followin' me, you nuts," he said.

"Okay," I said, "we're not gonna horse around no more. We'll sit here quietly."

We sat still for a while, then I giggled a little, but it wasn't the same as before. I was all giggled out. I felt like cryin', but I didn't. The train was gettin' full with people lookin' like they was gonna have a good time in Coney Island. They looked happy, and that made me sadder. I don' know why. Why when a person's sad, he wants other people to be sad also. It should be the other way, you know, but it isn't. Like if you see a friend who's havin' a hard time, they're down in the dumps, you try to cheer them up, and they get angry, right? They don' wanna be cheered up. They want you come down to the dumps with them. I guess when you're sad you feel alone. The whole world's against you. So if you see someone happy that just proves what you feel; that person's not with you, 'cause if he was, he'd be unhappy too.

The train filled up. We was swallowed up by a sea of people. So many people! They all rushed along like the waters of a flood, into the train, out of the rain. So many people, like if they was gatherin' for the judgement, and the Lord was comin' down on Coney Island. When we got there we got swept right out into the street with the rest of the crowd.

"Step right this way," said the devil.

"Hey, no man, I'm stayin' with my friends."

"Friends!" he said laughin'. "All right your friends can come along too. Step right this way and strap yourselves in."

"You look kind'a funny," I said to him.

"It's good for business," he answered.

"I mean I didn't expect you to look that way."

"Don' talk like that to the man," Gabi said.

"Don' worry about it," I said. "You can talk to devil any way you want. I mean, what difference does it make?"

Gabi seemed to think that over for a minute, then he said, "I guess you're right."

"Step right this way!" the man kept sayin' to people.

"Did you ever stop to think that the devil would be a music lover? Listen to that music! It's wonderful!"

"I think he knows his business."

"Hey Mario, are you all right?"

"I'm okay," I said.

In the bumper cars, we was drivin' down a long highway and all over there was bloody accidents. The road was black, and the line down the middle kept whizzin' by. Was the car movin' or was the line movin', no way to tell, ain't that a bitch! So here I was at the wheel drivin' at breakneck speed. I put my foot on the breaks. Nothin'! The brake pedal sank to the floor with no resistance. I've had it, I thought. This is the end. There was mutilated bodies right and left. The wreck of other cars was strewn all over the road. The car kept goin' with a mind of its own. I tried to steer around the wrecks. Jesus Christ! The steerin' wheel wouldn't respond. But that car, it didn't hit nothin'. That car was drivin' itself. It was drivin' itself faster and faster down the devil's road. There was somethin' directly in my path. I was prayin' this car was still lookin' where it was goin'. At first I couldn't see clearly what it was, then I realized it was Gabi in another car. I was gonna crash into Gabi.

"Get the hell out'a the way," I shouted, but he wasn't payin' no attention. Jesus Christ, I was gonna crash right into him. I couldn't break; I couldn't steer; it wasn't my fault. God it wasn't my fault! I crashed right smack into him. His car was demolished, but mine was okay. I felt somethin' wet on my face. I touched it. It was blood. I was splattered with blood. I looked on the road. Gabi's body was torn to pieces. It wasn't my fault. I killed my friend. The cars kept goin'. I thought the cops would come after me. It was hit and run. They would never believe that I couldn't stop the car.

The road became very narrow and windin' like a mountain road. I wasn't outdoors anymore. It was a road through a house. I was drivin' the car through a livin' room, then a basement, and up a narrow stairway. Back in the livin' room a woman was dustin'. I wondered whether she had noticed the blood on my face. I kept drivin'. Another car pulled up alongside mine. Gabi was drivin' it. Jesus Christ, I was relieved to see him alive. I wouldn't have to explain to the cops. "I thought you was dead," I said. "I'm glad I won't have to explain." "I'm not dead," he said. "Charlie's dead." Oh, my God! It was Charlie who got run over.

"Hey, Mario, are you all right?" Gabi shouted. He was steppin' out of a blue bumper car.

"You're alive," I said.

"Hell, yeah!"

"Let's go over to the carousel," Michelle said.

I looked at the devil. He was smilin'. I figured he wanted us to go over to the carousel, so I went. No matter where I am, I don' like to make no trouble.

"Let's get on," Michelle said.

"No, I don' wanna ride," I said.

"Oh, come on."

"No, you go," I said to them. "I'll watch from here." I was feelin' strange. I thought I might flip out if I was ridin' that damn thing. Gabi and Michelle got on. I just stood in the crowd and watched. As soon as the carousel began to turn, the people in the crowd began to shout insults at the riders. I didn't know what was goin' on. I looked around. The strangest thing was happenin'. The faces of the people around me was changin' to animal faces. Noses and mouths grew into snouts; ears became pointed and furry. They seemed horrible with their little animal eyes flashin' at those on the carousel. I panicked. I touched my own face. It was unrecognizable. I must'a've become like them. Yes! Now I understood. The people on the horses was escaping.

They was leaving us behind. They was riding away on them beautiful horses, riding into the sky. Michelle and Gabi, they were both getting away and leaving me. They was supposed to be my friends, but they was lookin' out only for themselves. They didn't care nothin' about me. I hated them, the hypocrites.

"Come back," I shouted. "Come back!" Laughing, they paid no attention to me. Maybe they didn't hear me. Maybe the carousel music was too loud. "Come back! Come back!" Next thing I knew we was on the Cyclone with Gabi. Up we went and down again. I felt sick. People were screaming everywhere.

"I wanna get off," I said.

"You can't get off now. You have to wait."

"I wanna get off. I'll jump."

"Don' be crazy. We got enough trouble."

"Let go of me," I said.

"Come on Mario, take it easy."

We was walkin' down one of the arcade alleys. It was crowded. I kept lookin' around for somebody. I knew there was somebody I had to find.

"There he is," I shouted, "over there!"

"Who?"

"The devil," I said.

"Where?"

"Over there, with the balloons."

"Jesus Christ, Mario that's just a man selling balloons."

"He's the devil! Can't you see? There he goes. He's leaving. There he goes into the sky."

"That's a balloon, Mario. A balloon got away from that little kid."

My eyes followed him. He was movinf down towards the parachute jump. "Come on let's watch what he does." We ran towards the parachute jump. "Look he's coming down," I said.

"The balloon busted. It must've hit against the rail up there. Yeah, that's what must've happened."

"It wasn't the devil at all," I shouted seeing my mistake. "Look, it's Charlie. He's falling."

"Jesus Christ, Mario, let's get out of there."

He hit the ground with a thud.

"There he is. He's bleeding! He's bleeding!"

"What are we gonna do? What are we gonna do?" Gabi asked Michelle.

They was worried about something. Only, I thought they was worried about Charlie, like I was.

"What are we gonna do? Nothing," I said. "There's nothing we can do now. He's dead."

"Let's take him home," Michelle said to Gabi.

"We can't do that," I said. "He's dead." I felt a lump in my throat. Then I started to cry. People was looking at us. I didn't wanna embarrass Michelle and Gabi, but I couldn't help it. I had'a cry. Michelle put her arms around me and hugged me. I was cryin' like a baby. She held me for a long time.

"You feel bad now," she said, "but it'll pass. You'll see, you'll feel better soon."

I looked up at the sky and around the crowd, the riders, the arcades. The noise of the motors was constant and mixed with the screams of thrill from the riders. Everywhere children and grownups was eatin' cotton candy, hot dogs, knishes. Mustard and catsup dripped from every mouth. This must be the worst day of my life, I thought. I took a couple'a steps backward and bumped into someone. He was a big guy, a real greaser. I didn't know there was none of them left. I thought they was all dirty hippies now.

"Why the fuck don't you watch where you're going," he said.

I felt like spittin' in his fat face, but he was bigger than me. His t-shirt was so tight I thought he was gonna bust out of it.

"Sorry," I said.

"Think sorry's gonna fix everything, wise guy?"

He buried his fist in my stomach. Pain shot up through my chest. I doubled over gaspin' for breath.

"Hey! Leave'm alone! He's sick!" Gabi shouted, comin' between the gorilla and me.

"He's gonna be a hospital case in a minute," the ape said, pushin' Gabi away.

The pain was still in my chest. I was tryin' to stand up straight, but it was hard. I didn't wanna let him see how hurt I was. I could feel the tears comin' up.

"You fuck'n ape," I said, "don' you be pushin' my friend."

"Why you dirty Spic I'm gonna knock the shit out of you."

"You better get away before you have to be carried away," I said. I don' know why I said that. I would get creamed in a fight.

"We can't fight here," he said. "You wanna fight me, you come on under the boardwalk."

"He don' wanna fight nobody," Gabi said. "He said he's sorry. Let's forget it."

"You don' have to protect me, man," I said. "I can take on this ape shit any time."

"Keep talking Spic. You're talking your way right into your coffin."

"Come on Mario, let's go," Michelle said to me.

"Turn and run you yellow cocksucker."

I rushed at him. I was really mad then. He blocked my blow and started movin' towards the boardwalk.

"Not here, not here," he said. "You wanna die? Come on over this way."

Under the boardwalk I made a grab for his throat. I felt my nails sink into him. Then a terrible blow to the side of my head stunned me. I felt there was no use fightin' him, but couldn't retreat. His face was all red and puffed up. I wished I could step on it with hobnail boots. I kept hittin' him, and he kept hittin' me. I wondered if he felt any pain. I was ready to die. A crowd gathered. I wished someone would stop the fight, but there was little chance of that. It seemed to me everyone was cheerin'm on. Then for some reason he fell, and I saw my chance. I was down on him, hittin' his face as hard as I could. Someone jumped me from behind. I wanted to pulverize the one on the ground, but the one on my back was really hurtin' me.

I heard Gabi shout, "You dirty guinea, that's not fair!"

Someone threw sand in my eyes just after I saw Gabi go down, two guys beatin' on him. I tried to rub the sand out of my eyes, but that made them sting all the more. I felt blood drippin' over my lips. I could hardly see, but I looked around for somethin' to use as a weapon, a stick or somethin'—a bottle. Next thing I knew I had a knife in my hand. All I saw was the hand of the guy who passed it to me. I didn't get a glimpse of his face till later. The knife had a long blade and a smooth green handle. It felt good in my hand, the smooth handle. I could just see the blade turn red, dripping with blood. My first thought was to throw it away. What if I killed somebody? But I didn't throw it away. I stood there holdin' it.

"Hey, he's got a knife," someone shouted.

I stood there waitin' for them to come at me, but they didn't. They must've taken off. I couldn't see them. The crowd began to disperse. Gabi, he was gettin' up from the sand. His face was bleedin'. I was numb. I stood there holdin' the knife. Then in a fit of rage I fell on my knees and stabbed the ground over and over again.

"I'm gonna kill them motherfuckers. I'm gonna kill them," I said sobbin'. The sand flew in all directions as the knife went wildly in and out.

"Take it easy, Mario," Michelle came over to me with tissue and started wipin' the blood from my face. I flinched a little.

"I'm sorry," she said. "I'll try to be careful."

"That's all right," I said. I could hardly move my lips. "Take care of Gabi."

The guy who had given me the knife was standin' by. I guess he wanted his knife back. I handed it to him. "Thanks," I said.

"Anytime," he said smilin'. He was a long thin person. One of his eyes was brown and the other blue; a couple of his teeth had gold caps. "You better get out of here before they come back," he said.

"Yeah, let's go home," Michelle said.

The man took us to the subway.

"Thanks again," I said.

"You're okay," Michelle said, and she shook his hand.

It was a long ride home. I never felt worse in all my life.

8

It was dark when I got home. I was glad that nobody was hangin' out on the stoop, so I wouldn't have to explain about the bumps on my face. The light was out in the hallway. It was almost pitch black in there. My brother and sister were watchin' TV when I walked in . My father wasn't home. I figured my mother was in her room prayin'. I tried to hurry through the livin' room, before they would look up and start askin' me questions.

"Hey, what's the matter with you?" my brother piped up. My sister didn't take her eyes off the TV.

"Nothin'," I said. I hurried to my room. He followed me. It was his room too.

"What happened?"

"Well, what does it look like?"

"You got beat up. That's what it looks like."

"If you know the answer, stop askin' stupid questions."

"You don' have to get mad," he said.

I didn't say nothin', 'cause he was right.

"There's food for you on the stove."

"I'm not hungry," I said.

"You look hungry. I'll brin' it to you."

He brought back some rice and beans.

"How did it happen?"

"Some guys jumped me."

"Where?"

"Coney Island?"

"Coney Island! You went to Coney Island?"

I could see he was disappointed that I hadn't taken him along. "It wasn't like you think," I said. "It wasn't a fun trip."

"Where was you last night?"

"Over at Andy Coto's."

"You shouldn't hang out with people like that. They'll get you in trouble."

"I can take care of myself," I said, but I didn't feel too good about sayin' it, 'cause my bruised face was proof that I couldn't.

"You gonna tell ma?"

"Nah, she'll just get upset."

"Well, she's gonna see you sooner or later."

"I'll be better by tomorrow."

"You'll be black and blue."

I heard my mother come out of her room and tell my sister to turn off the TV and go to bed.

"Mario's home," my sister said.

My mother came to the door. Norberto had bolted it.

"Are you in there, Mario?"

"Yeah," I said.

"Where were you last night? How many times do you want me to tell you? You have to come home every night." She didn't sound too angry.

"I was at a party, and I fell asleep," I said. "I didn't mean to."

"Alright," she said. She sounded tired.

I wanted to open the door, but I didn't want her to see me all beat up. Why should I be so much grief to her? I was glad my brother was more sensible than me. He stayed out of trouble mostly. She went to turn off the TV. My sister started to cry. Every night was the same thin'. My sister wanted to watch TV all night. I think there's somethin' wrong with her.

"Did you hear about that guy Charlie?" my brother asked.

"Yeah, I heard."

"At least you're luckier than him," he said.

"Yeah, I guess so."

When I finished the rice and beans, I gave Norberto the plate to take back to the kitchen. I lay in my bed with my eyes open for long time. There was a crack in the ceiling where the plaster was fallin' out. Every time someone walked in the apartment above some plaster fell into our room. I studied the crack every night. It was like an old friend—like if it had a personality or somethin'. It was frightenin', but it had been over us so long that I was used to it mostly. But sometimes I was still scared. It reminded me of an old man who had gotten ugly from doin' evil deeds—all his sins showed on his face. Sometimes I thought my guardian angel had left me, and the scar on the ceilin' had taken his place.

When I thought that, I really got frightened, 'cause if I died that old face could take me to only one place, and I didn't wanna go there.

I heard mice scurrying around on the floor. I hated that sound—their little feet hurrying across the linoleum. I knew they wouldn't come on the bed while I was sleeping, but I hated to hear them. I could never get used to them, like I could get used to other things. It's funny how sometimes it's the little problems that get to you. Anyway, I laid there in bed wondering whether I should go to Charlie's funeral. Maybe I shouldn't go. I mean, after all, he was dead, so what difference would it make. My going wouldn't make him happy, and it would just make me very sad. So why go? I thought I wouldn't go, but then I got to thinking that it was my duty to go. Charlie was my friend, and just for that I had to go to his funeral.

All night I kept hearing the mice. There was no way to get rid of them. I once tried setting traps, but after the first few got caught, the rest stayed away from them. I put poison out, but they wouldn't eat it. They was pretty smart those mice. A while back someone offered me a cat, but I couldn't keep it on account of my asthma, besides they stink up the place something awful, and who needs another mouth to feed? Well, what can you do? That's life. I stayed up a long time trying to figure out how to get rid of the mice. I came up with nothing.

www.ingramcontent.com/pod-product-compliance
Lightning Source LLC
LaVergne TN
LVHW090944080826
845145LV00003B/884

9780979598685